HELL ON EARTH

REALITY BLEED BOOK 9

J.Z. FOSTER

WINTER GATE PUBLISHING

For MIBLART, my Ukrainian cover artist who have produced such beautiful works.

They produced these covers under a Russian invasion, and never expressed a single complaint.

My heart breaks for them.

PROLOGUE

*T**HE** R**ED** B**ITCH** of Berlin was dead.*

The word spread through the Soviet forces like wildfire, but for the moment, that didn't matter to Maslov.

He was hunting the Janissary.

"*Go,*" he said over a closed comm link, gesturing with his fingers.

His team of black and red CAG soldiers moved toward the mouth of a cave. A downpouring of rain peppered their armor and turned the dirt into slop, making them leave tracks.

Two hours ago, air recon had discovered a location where Soviet intelligence determined a small group of cronux were taking shelter. The signs of deliberate movement as if to hide their numbers was unusual for the cronux.

Intelligence believed it to be a high-value target.

The Janissary.

Maslov's team was deployed to go in and confirm, and if correct, destroy the targets.

Even with the *Berlin Bitch* dead, the war continued.

The unit spread out and moved in a leapfrog formation, with some taking cover while others aimed their rifles. They moved like ghosts, with quick but quiet movements, and armor designed to reduce noise.

Each man nestled into a spot behind the rocks and watched, carefully waiting for Maslov's orders.

It was dark—well after midnight—but Maslov's helmet took in ambient light and illuminated a clear gray screen even with the rain. A green readout blinked in the corner of the helmet screen displaying temperature and a feed on his rifle's current ammunition. He looked along the ridges of the cave and out along the coastline as the dark waters lapped up to the beach.

Nothing.

"Alpha, take position," he ordered.

"Confirmed."

A single, slender soldier broke away from the group and moved to the mouth of the cave, her rifle aimed into the darkness.

She knelt down and scanned back and forth.

Her voice buzzed over the feed. *"No target, but tracks in the dirt. There was movement here."*

Maslov glanced toward the ground around himself. Not a single clear track that wasn't one of their own.

They'd hidden it.

They were smart.

He pressed his call button.

"Weapons hot, we're heading in."

Each soldier responded. *"Confirmed."*

"Delta proceed."

Two soldiers broke away and moved toward the mouth, joining Alpha. The others scanned the ridgelines, prepared for an ambush.

None came.

Moments later, a man's voice came on.

"Target spotted."

"Send feed," Maslov ordered.

A second later, a square vidfeed opened up in Maslov's helmet screen, and he could see what the soldier saw. Maslov narrowed his eyes, activating facial commands, and the screen zoomed.

A large limbed creature knelt toward a rock wall, its back faced toward them, completely still.

2

It was the Janissary. He could tell by how tall and slender it was compared to the others.

Others with smaller, but similar shapes surrounded the Janissary. Their bodies lay collapsed onto the floor or knelt against the walls.

Maslov watched for a moment, but didn't see any kind of movement.

"*Hold position,*" he ordered and then pressed call buttons on his gauntlet, connecting his voice to the command channel.

"*Command, do you read?*"

An officer overseeing the mission responded. "*Confirmed Viper leader, you are connected with Command, go ahead.*"

"*Target confirmed but appears nonhostile. Requesting orders.*"

"*Viper leader, proceed in and investigate. Engage when hostile.*"

"*Confirmed,*" Maslov reconnected to the squad channel.

He didn't like any of this. It didn't feel right.

Too easy.

He scanned the ridge again looking for any sign of movement.

Still none.

"*Eyes wide Delta team. Alpha, proceed in and investigate. Send feed.*"

"*Confirmed.*"

Delta's feed shrank and Alpha's feed popped below it. Maslov watched as Alpha proceeded forward, his eyes glancing up and down between the two before settling on Alpha's feed. He could see the nose of her rifle, and even the other two squad members as they moved within her peripheral vision.

Maslov closed the eye with the feeds and used the other to focus on the ridge.

Something was about to happen, he felt it in his bones.

Something terrible.

He opened the other eye and focused on Delta's screen.

The soldiers slowed to a crawl as they moved up to the large kneeling creature.

Nothing moved.

"*Get me visual of targets,*" Maslov ordered.

"*Confirmed.*"

3

The video feed fanned across the creatures.

All still, their faces twisted in pain with skin dry and cracked.

Alpha moved in close to the Janissary.

She held out her rifle further and Maslov could see her hand on the forward grip loosen and tighten in anticipation. She pressed the rifle barrel into the back of the Janissary's head.

It cracked in the flesh like it was dry plaster.

Dark blood rolled out like a thick oil, with chunks of flesh.

"The fuck . . ." the soldier whispered as she reached her hand out onto the Janissary's shoulder. She pulled back and the Janissary's torso cracked off and fell to the ground, breaking into pieces, while the legs stayed frozen in a kneeling position. Blood clots oozed up with the dark oil from the openings.

"Eyes wide, eyes wide," Maslov cautioned.

His hands squeezed onto the rifle.

Alpha's feed focused on the Janissary's face.

It was wrinkled and dry like old fruit, the lips sucked in and cracked.

Maslov pressed a finger to his gauntlet and clicked. His extra feed switched to another soldier looking down at a kneeling cronux, one arm under its chin, the other snapped off and on the ground.

Maslov pressed the button again and the feed switched to the third soldier scanning over all the dead cronux.

"They're dead. They're all dead," the soldier said.

Something had happened here.

Something terrible.

1

RICHARD JOHN ROLES sat behind a thick layer of glass and watched a man on the other side.

Jeremiah Johnson.

Army Ranger.

Medically retired.

Johnson had the unfortunate luck of being in the wrong place at the wrong time and catching a heat bomb that melted through his CAG.

The heat had been so intense that it fused pieces of the metal to Johnson's body.

The doctors had to remove both legs and an arm with a copious amount of skin tissue.

The Soviets had surely supplied that heat bomb, but that was the old news of yesterday; now the U.S. was quickly implementing the *Garin Doctrine,* named after the current Soviet Grand Marshal, Sergei Garin—the only military officer outside of Alice Winters who had any real success with combating the cronux.

But that was neither here nor there at the moment.

Right now, Roles was focused on Jeremiah Johnson.

After having his legs removed, the Army paid for a brand new set and even threw in the arm, but things were never the same. Johnson's body had reacted poorly. The doctors say that having that many new mechanized limbs can sometimes overload the brain as they build new pathways.

It dulls the reflexes.

There was no shortage of soldiers with replacement limbs within the U.S. military, but a soldier might be fine to lose a foot, an arm, or even peel off a few fingers.

But losing nearly half the body?

That made a man damaged goods.

So, while Johnson's mind was as sharp as ever, his body was no longer Ranger quality.

Or some would think.

Not Roles—he could see the potential.

He'd said as much just days ago when he'd called the man, with a datapad in hand showing Johnson's scarred body.

Roles made his pitch.

"Medically retired, but you exercise, and still wear a clean shave. I'd bet you even make your bed every morning."

"Yes sir, I do."

"That's the kind of man that the country needs right now, son. A man with the scars of life but still makes his bed every morning. Are you that man?"

"Yes sir, I am."

That confirmation, and a few signed documents, and the deal was sealed.

They were in a military research facility twelve floors below ground now, and Johnson was stripped down to his underwear and behind a thick layer of protective glass. Roles could see all of the scars and connected mechanized limbs, like a jigsaw puzzle with some extra pieces thrown in that happened to fit.

Roles looked past the scars and watched for any sign of fear.

There was none.

"Tell him to go in."

A technician at a desk nodded and leaned forward to the microphone. "Please head into the room."

Johnson moved to stand in front of the door as it slid into the wall. Chilled air rolled out of the room. Johnson's skin prickled as he entered into a large metal tank not unlike a room within a space shuttle. A doctor in a hazmat suit greeted him inside and gestured toward a chair that looked like one that could be found in a dentist's office.

The door closed and locked in place with a flash of green light and a confident beep.

Sensitive microphones were set into the walls, and Roles could hear the groaning of Johnson's mechanized limbs as he moved to take a seat.

Each breath was visible in the cold air, as it was necessary to keep the room cold.

It made the specimens more docile.

"Someone get me a coffee," Roles said without so much a glance backward.

The doctor worked straps over Johnson's body and tightened them down while Johnson stared at the ceiling.

When the doctor finished, he gave a thumbs-up to the mirror.

Roles rubbed his chin and stared.

The technician cleared his throat. "They're ready."

Roles agreed and kept his eyes on Johnson.

The man was a patriot.

He hadn't hesitated a moment when Roles explained to him what they were going to do—the hell Roles wanted to put him in.

He'd gone through Ranger school, fought in war, got blown up, and spent hundreds of hours in rehab to be here, at this moment, once again answering the call for his country.

He was a warrior in every sense of the word.

A patriot.

Roles cleared his throat.

"Begin."

The technician pressed a button and spoke, "Proceed."

The doctor in the hazmat suit gave another thumbs-up and

grabbed a small cart. He wheeled it close to the chair, and the squeak of the wheels resounded loudly over the speakers.

"Someone dial down the sensitivity on the microphones, I don't need to hear them pass gas," Roles ordered.

He picked up a scalpel and leaned toward Johnson's one remaining arm, just below the elbow.

That's where Alice Winters had gotten it.

Someone tapped Roles on the arm and he glanced back. A technician offered a steaming styrofoam cup of coffee.

Roles took the cup and blew on it as the doctor pressed the tip of the blade down in Johnson's arm. Johnson inhaled sharply as a bead of blood welled up, but did nothing else.

The doctor leaned down to the wound and used his fingers to spread it wider.

Blood oozed.

Roles took a sip.

Johnson didn't look any more than mildly discomforted as he focused on the ceiling, though he certainly felt every bit of discomfort. They hadn't given him any painkillers. They needed his mind sharp.

The doctor in the hazmat suit turned away and brought a canister over.

The same kind the Chinese had used in their *Dragonskin* program. The Chinese weren't the only ones stealing secrets.

But what did it really matter?

The Chinese only had one success.

But that was one more than Roles.

Johnson couldn't see it, but Roles stared into his eyes. There was a closeness when meeting one's gaze, and if nothing else, Roles would be there to watch Johnson's eyes, even if it was behind a glass wall.

Roles ordered, "Do it." He took another sip.

The technicians hit the microphone button, and Roles vaguely heard them talking, but his attention was on Johnson.

The doctor with the hazmat suit gave a thumbs-up and twisted the top of the canister.

A cool mist poured out like dry ice.

The doctor sat the lid aside and held the open canister to Johnson's wound.

Thin wisps spiraled out in slow, rhythmic gestures. The cold had done its work to slow them.

The fat lump pulled up to the edge and Roles felt an odd twist in his stomach.

The parasite looked like a small kidney with loose, saggy flesh. Its wisps snaked out until a tip slid across Johnson's wounds.

The wisps snapped toward it and hooked inside his wound.

Johnson's eyes flared open as the fat parasite leapt from the cage and toward the open wound.

It sank quicker than Roles could have imagined, and the strands slid beneath Johnson's skin, the edges poking up like fingers beneath a sheet.

Johnson hissed and reflexively tightened against his restraints. His body spasmed and shook as the parasite disappeared into the wound.

Roles held still, steaming cup in his hand.

This was the moment where it would happen—where Jeremiah Johnson would conquer the parasite . . .

Or succumb to it.

Johnson's mouth widened enough that his heart could have crawled out, but he only made a deep bellowing moan as the veins pulsed in his neck.

The restraint groaned as Johnson twisted and rolled, the fingers on his hands curling like claws.

There was an intense struggle happening within the man, one that could determine the fate of the world.

"Do it. Now," Roles barked.

The technician spoke and the doctor closed in with a syringe. He bent over close to the wound and stuck the needle in, pumping cryo into the parasite.

Johnson's back softened, but his fingers tightened. His eyes rolled back into his skull.

Roles let out his breath with a muffled sigh.

He kept his eyes forward. He owed Johnson that.

9

Roles knew what was happening.

He was watching Johnson die.

They'd failed. How? Why? Roles didn't know, but he'd seen it before.

He would see it again.

Jeremiah Johnson was not the first, and he would not be the last in the *Ghost Initiative*.

There were always more patriots with blood to spill.

Johnson's body rolled and squirmed like a person trying to see how a new pair of pants fit. And when his head tilted forward, Roles could see his cold, dead eyes.

He wasn't a man anymore.

He was a monster.

"Kill it," Roles ordered.

The technicians gave his orders, but Roles didn't stay to watch. He only turned around and looked at his crew.

"Clean it up and bring the next one in."

2

THERE ARE moments in history when powers rise and fall.

When the lines on the globe shift.

Now was such a time.

With the world distracted, it was time to take a step forward, and to settle old debts.

Zhao stood tall, his hands folded behind his back, and the soft glow of the digital world map lit his face.

A general gestured with one hand at the screen, and a series of red dots moved across the map. "With the West occupied, we believe conventional forces could seize our ancestral lands in Korea, and push our boundaries with Burma. India has drawn down its Eastern forces to deal with an outbreak in New Delhi and our forces there have already expanded our border into the mountains. Vietnam has requested our assistance and—"

Zhao interrupted, "Our Dragon will assist Vietnam after he's dealt with Mongolia if Vietnam agrees to withdraw its protest of our sea claims."

"Sir, they've already agreed."

"No, that was the previous offer, and the deal has changed. If they want our assistance, then they will have to negotiate the extent of the access to the seas. And we will offer assistance to India after we dispatch our trade minister to settle our new economic agreements in conjunction with their withdrawal from our territorial claims. The Dragon will travel there only when the ink is dry on our agreements of the border lines."

The general bowed his head. "Mongolia has also requested a cease in hostilities. They've agreed to surrender to our territorial claims and offered to renegotiate terms of trade."

Zhao stared at the screen. There was a blue glow casted onto his eyes as he watched the dots spread across Mongolia.

He imagined what that map might have looked like in centuries past, when the Mongolians would raid Chinese towns, taking slaves and riches at their leisure.

The women were useful to them; the men and children were not.

Chroniclers found the bodies piled so high that the melted fat became toxic to breathe.

It was long ago, but China still bore the scars and did not easily forget such horrors.

Zhao would see justice enacted.

"There will be no peace with Mongolia. Not for the evils they committed against us. We will use them as an example to the world of the power of our Dragon."

"Yes sir," the general said, his back bent and his head down. "And what of the West? They have opened lines of communication."

"When all of our debts are settled, and old feuds repaid, China will answer the call to save the world." Zhao's eyes moved to America and watched the red dots infesting New York. "Until then, we will let the pot boil."

MUD SUCKED at Erkin Kahn's boot as he walked through the streets of Zamyn-Uud, a Mongolian city on the border with China. His skin prickled as the cold rain pelted him. It was pouring enough to be blinding, but his CAG helmet had receptors that kept his screen clear and visible.

He was cold, but that was not a problem.

It was the screaming that disturbed him.

It was little comfort that their words were all in Mongolian, and he couldn't understand them. He could tell by the shrills that they were dying painfully.

But still, he had his arms out as he walked, his palms open to the sky while the rain hit his bare skin. Though his hands were empty, with his mind they held the horde, and they obeyed his command.

Kill. Feed.

A wave of cronux flooded through the city akin to ants swarming a corpse, and Erkin was with each one, and he saw what they saw, for in this world, he had many eyes.

With each death, the hordes' numbers grew, and Erkin's mind stretched further.

He saw a man running for his life, only to stumble and fall as the wave rolled over him, shredding his body in seconds. A clustered group of holdout soldiers fired at the horde, and Erkin felt the impact of the bullets, though to him it wasn't even an itch.

There were no tactics or strategy as they flooded over the soldiers, tearing apart their armor and gear. They left so little that many of the bodies could not be reanimated.

But some still rose.

Women with a hundred bite marks and open flesh.

A man with a confused heart that was still beating caused blood to spray from a neck wound as he joined Erkin's control.

More and more still.

Erkin's hands were empty, but they were heavy.

Erkin took another step, his boot sliding in the mud, and heard the calls of the dying as the cronux dragged bodies to him as if to devour the meat in his presence was some strange form of worship.

Chinese aircraft screamed overhead, though they were not necessary. Mongolia did not have the air power to resist, but this was never about war.

Mongolia and China had long had border disputes and negotiations over mineral rights, but their feud went beyond such petty disagreements.

Their feud was ancient.

Erkin knew this, but it was an idea that shifted just beyond close inspection, as if it existed in a fog, and he could only touch it for moments.

It was hard to think.

It was easy to obey.

Erkin planted a foot before him and lifted his hand high, and all around him the cronux madness sharpened.

3

JOHN WINTERS RUBBED at his eye as he sat down on a cold metal chair. His eye had a nasty twitch that wouldn't stop. With a sigh, he rolled up the sleeve on one arm and propped it on the table.

A stone-faced doctor slipped on plastic gloves, but John barely noticed.

He was too busy thinking of Alice.

Things were moving so quickly that he didn't have time to focus. But it was in the little quiet moments, like this, that it all settled on him.

His little girl was dead.

When he first heard, it hit him like a nail in the heart. A strange disillusioned sense of feeling like he had to do something to bring her back clouded over him.

Could he rip out his heart to bring her back?

Could he fall to his knees and plead with God?

He'd felt that feeling before when he got the news of Alice's mother, his wife's, passing.

It was a poor thing for a man to outlive a wife.

Even worse to outlive a daughter.

The doctor grabbed his wrist and stretched out John's arm. He turned John's hand faceup and tapped just below the pit of the elbow, looking for a vein.

"There it is," the doctor's tone was stale. He pulled out a syringe and John watched as he plunged it into the vein.

A thick, warm liquid entered into John's bloodstream—a stimulant to keep him up and aware. His third so far.

Side effects include a nervous twitch in the eyes.

Fortunately, it was just the one eye for John.

He rubbed it again.

He'd been awake for more than thirty-five hours, but who was counting?

Alice had given her life to the war.

John would honor the sacrifice by doing his part.

"That knock the rust off?" Roles asked, standing just a few feet away.

John squeezed his hand into a fist to help work the stimulant through his system.

"Yeah."

"We're going to have to talk about New York." Roles crossed his arms over his chest.

John glanced over to the doctor and gave him a silent nod. The man gathered his things, and left the two in the quiet room.

"I just spent eighteen hours in the situation room, Roles. You know everything I know about New York. The military is deploying what they can. They'll try and hold it back while we prepare the offensive."

"They'll fail. It'll spread," Roles said, still standing.

John rubbed his temple and pointed at a chair. "Can you at least sit down, or would you like me to stand?"

Roles grabbed a chair and dragged it across the ground with a scratch to sit across from John. He thumbed back to the situation room. "Half of them want to nuke New York."

"You think I wasn't there? We've all seen what happened in the Soviet Union, what's happening in Europe." John gestured toward the door that led to the situation room. "We've got a twenty-four-hour feed on the slaughterhouse in New York. Goddammit Roles, I know people there."

"No value in having any personal attachment to the situation."

"If you came here to tell me I shouldn't be the one making these calls, then I'd agree with you. But I don't have a choice, and I'm sure as hell not giving you the job."

Roles snorted. "I don't want the job. But I have more concerns than the military does."

"Roles, no one knows where the hell McAndrews is. I can't remember the last time I slept or ate anything, and I just stepped out of that room so I could come in here and think about what to do with Europe. You know they're begging us for troops? They're saying we only have *one* outbreak while the whole European Federation is looking at a full-scale ground war. And the Chinese are pushing their leverage. They're on the move, and when I ask Zhao about assistance, the best I get is *in time*. So I have concerns too."

"China will come around. They just want to let us soften up, and then swoop in. They see it as payback for old transgressions."

"Yeah, old transgressions no one alive today had anything to do with."

Roles made a face like there was a bad smell. "Something's amiss, and I don't think the military will hold it down, even with nuclear weapons. That hadn't worked in Moscow. I want to send an agent in to look into things."

"Look into things? They're just as likely to get killed up there."

"Maybe. She knows the risks. But she's smart, and she was able to go in and out of the Soviet Union. Deep into it. She's closer to this than anyone else."

John's eyes sharpened. "You're talking about Moller? The member of Orbital Corp that was on Felicity with my daughter?"

Roles nodded. "As of right now, she's one of the leading experts on the cronux, both tactical and biological. She's seen them up close more than anyone else. We also want to field-test the new weapons."

"This the irradiated armor I've gotten reports on?"

Roles nodded.

17

"Long Island is one hundred miles long. You want her to run around on foot? What the hell kind of good is that going to do?"

"She'll need a drop and an extraction."

"Fine, but honestly, I don't know why you're asking me. You sure as hell haven't asked me for permission for anything else."

Roles sucked in a breath and stared into John's eyes. He folded his hands in front of him and straightened his back.

"Because I want her to take your grandson."

4

"*This isn't my first rodeo, Moller.*"

Roles's voice had the crackle of a man who hadn't slept in days.

"*We ask him to take the boy to New York, and we settle for you to go talk to him. Make it count.*"

Those were the orders she'd received. From what she was told, John Winters practically killed Roles on the spot, but the plan had worked.

Moller was going to talk with the boy.

And now, she squeezed her hands behind her back as she waited at the door of the White House residential rooms.

The ornate door opened to a dimly lit room with the windows covered, and a faint smell of disinfectant rolled out.

First Lady, Cora Winters, Alice's stepmother, held the door.

She glowered at Moller. "You're the one that was on Felicity with Alice, aren't you?"

"Yes."

"And you're here only to talk, yes?" Her face was stiff.

"Yes."

"He's been through a lot, you understand that right?"

"We all have," Moller agreed.

"Then why do you want to talk to him?"

Moller had been calm, but now she let her gaze settle on Cora's. "You know why."

There was a moment of silence before Cora stepped aside. "He's down the hall. I keep it dark. The light seems to bother him."

A single lamp was all that lit the room. Moller entered and forced her hands to her side.

"*Wait*," Cora said and closed the door behind her. Her face softened and she stepped closer to Moller. "You were Alice's friend weren't you? The two of you were close?"

Moller nodded. "She saved my life. More than once."

Cora's eyes glistened, but her voice stayed steady. "Then be careful with him. He's not like other children."

Moller gave a thin, sympathetic grin. "I know."

Cora shook her head. "No, no. I don't think you do. He's smarter than other children. Much smarter. Sometimes he talks like he's a college student, and other times like a child. And the way he looks at people." Cora turned her eyes from Moller. "I love him. I do. But you should know. He's *different*." Cora looked up again, and now a tear rolled down her face. "Be gentle, he just lost his mother after all, and he's been saying . . . strange things."

"I'll be gentle," Moller said and Cora walked away.

Moller headed down the long, dark hallway and to the room at the end of the hall.

The floorboards groaned with each step as she came to the door and reached for the handle. She stopped.

Someone was whispering inside, but it was hard to hear.

Moller looked back to Cora, but she wasn't there anymore, so Moller put her ear to the door.

"*Three by three, and nothing more . . . One to none, and then the fun. Break the back and eat the dead. The king will laugh, but has no head. The party then is such a bore. So now we say . . . three by three and nothing more.*"

Moller's skin prickled as she leaned back. She'd never heard a rhyme like that, and wasn't sure if she got it all.

She put her ear to the door again, but there was a sudden thumping of feet upon the floor.

Moller pulled back as something smacked into the door.

It opened with a creek and Eli was there.

"Hello," he didn't whisper now, but spoke like a child. He opened it wider and Moller could see he was wearing a formal jacket and shirt, but was standing in his underwear and dragging a teddy bear by the leg. The underwear had urine stains.

Moller straightened up. "Eli, I was a friend of your mother. I want to talk to you some."

"About the monsters?" he asked without concern.

"Yes, but Eli, who were you talking to?"

Eli craned his head forward, then glanced back into his room.

He fixed her with a stare.

"Myself."

Moller looked into the room, but it was too dark to see inside.

"Do you want to come in?" Eli pushed the door and the shadows crept back as the light from the hallway entered.

Moller hesitated but walked inside. The room smelled like piss.

Eli started to shut the door, but Moller snatched the edge and held it.

"Leave it open. I won't be here long." She leaned down and Eli's eyes watched her the whole way. "I want to talk to you about what you're seeing, Eli."

"You want to know about my mother? What I say to her?"

"No, not your mother, Eli. I know what happened to her."

Eli frowned and twisted his head. He put a finger up on his bottom lip and flicked it to make it pop. "What happened to her?"

Moller hesitated. Cora said he knew. Had he forgotten? Was it a game? "Eli, your mother died."

"*Died?*" Eli raised a lip, showing teeth. "She's not dead."

The words caught in Moller's throat. She'd never heard a child talk that way.

Eli took a step closer, and Moller took one back.

"*He* has her." He licked his lips and grinned. "But he promised to give her back."

5

ALICE SAT up in her chair and rubbed a hand over her forehead. She was having a terrible migraine.

It felt like something was crawling around inside her skull.

She reached over to the shelf and grabbed a pill bottle. Half fogged with exhaustion, she screwed off the top and dropped out two pills. She swallowed them dry and leaned back into the seat.

She needed to sleep. A few good hours and the migraine might subside.

But how could she sleep when the floor kept moving?

The floorboards rose and fell like they were taking a breath. Alice let out a sigh and looked out the window.

Black veins crawled across the glass, and they oozed with blood.

This place was alive.

The arms of the chair curled as if to draw Alice in, but she pushed back, demanding it keep shape.

None of this seemed particularly strange, only annoying. But there was something about it . . .

Get up, Alice. Get out of here.

That was a voice coming from somewhere. She leaned up, but doing so made her head hurt all the worse.

She tried to move, but then again, why get up at all when her head hurt so bad? Why do anything but lay back down into the chair . . .

And drift away?

The chair began to recline and Alice's eyes felt heavy. The pulsing veins on the window and the heaving of the floor were all the more rhythmic to put her to sleep.

The arms of the chair oozed up her shoulders, forming a grip.

A vague thought came to her. Why was she even here? Where was this place?

Alice . . .

There was that voice again.

Alice . . . if you don't leave now . . .

Her eyes fluttered open once more.

It's going to take you.

Alice leaned up from the chair, but it bit her.

She shrieked and looked down to see the arms of the chair had grown hundreds of teeth. They cut into her side. She felt a tongue slurp up her backside as it moved to swallow her.

Alice thrashed and screamed until she got an arm loose. She grabbed onto the window sill and pulled.

Her body came up, and pieces of skin tore off her arms.

Alice pulled from the chair and thumped onto the heaving floor; her blood ran down her sides.

She looked back to see the chair was a mouth with a lashing tongue. She got up from the floor as the chair started to come toward her.

Alice scrambled to her feet and went to the door of the room. She yanked it open only to see the hallway was a mouth with gnashing teeth.

She backed away as the chair hobbled toward her, its jaws snapping.

Alice looked around the room and saw the window.

She ran and dove through it.

ALICE WOKE up cold and screaming.

Or she tried to scream, but her throat was full.

Something was in her eyes, and she was blind. Her left arm was stuck, but with her right, she grabbed the thing hanging from her mouth. Her fingers sunk into soft flesh with thin hair bristles. She pulled, but her grip slid on the creature's wet skin. She gripped harder and pulled more.

It wiggled and scratched as it came out of her throat and she gagged as it came loose.

She hurled it away and turned to her trapped arm. She yanked but it felt like tearing skin.

Grinding her teeth, she pulled harder and felt flesh tear.

It shouldn't have. That arm was the replacement.

She rolled and fell off a table.

Still blind, she stumbled to her feet, but she was shaking and cold, and there was a blistering pain from the open wound on her stump of an arm. She rubbed her eyes and saw blurs in the room.

Glowing cronux crawled along the wall like fat worms with legs that clicked.

The thing from her throat hissed and squirmed on the floor.

Gasping, she reached around until she found something to grab onto for balance.

She moved forward on trembling legs, but to where, she didn't know.

Something growled or burped behind her and Alice moved quicker.

She smacked into a wall and stumbled back.

A wave of sickness rolled up from her stomach and her head pounded.

She was too dizzy to stand, too weak to do anything but lay there and breathe.

Then she felt him.

Their minds touched and she could feel his presence in the room.

The Archon.

His steps thumped onto the floor. Her heart pounded in her chest.

She wiped her eyes again, but there was still a fog.

She barely saw him approach.

"A-wake?" he said, the words awkward in his throat. Alice scrambled back but he grabbed and lifted her into the air. "*Come—*"

"No! No!"

"*—to me.*"

He grabbed around her throat, his fingers squeezing hard enough to choke. Alice gasped and struggled for air. She clawed at his wrists, but it was like scratching stone.

He thumped her onto the table and smashed her elbow back down to where it was. Alice looked over to see reaching veins reconnect into her stump.

She was growing a new arm.

He pushed her head back and grabbed the squirming worm from the floor.

Alice struggled but he shoved it in between her teeth and it snaked down her throat.

"*Sleep,*" the Archon hissed and pushed her head back.

Alice struggled, and clawed at the worm, but the Archon put one hand on her chest, and the other at her throat.

"*In time.*"

He squeezed.

"*You will wake.*"

THE ARCHON WAS BRED to be a god. Born from the Mother, he was one of the few blessed with her voice and her gifts.

His being was beyond that of the others. He was not born to lead, he was born to be worshiped.

This world was his to seize, along with all within it.

But there was something strange that stirred in him. A desire unreflected by any of his children, or even his brothers.

He desired beauty—a concept unknown to any of the others.

And he desired the woman.

Now, within the cold tomb of some destroyed military facility, he kept her there in near-total darkness.

And though he didn't need the light, he desired that too.

He wanted to see her.

Cronux that glowed with neon light crawled around the walls, and their green shades bathed her.

He watched her body on the table as it changed. One of his children had crawled up to her stump of an arm, and died there, letting its malleable body fuse to her.

A gift from the Archon, a new arm to replace the one she'd lost. He saw the gray-flesh arm quivering and moving as it bonded to her body. Dark purple veins crawled up it and slid beneath her skin. They moved up her body, and even now, the Archon could see them digging deeper into her face, around the eye, and into her brain.

But the body was an easy thing to break and change.

It was the mind that was hard to break.

And hers was strong—she'd even thrown off his reins and woken up.

It only made him desire her all the more.

He came now to focus, and draw her deeper in.

———

ALICE OPENED HER EYES. Her blonde hair was wet and stuck to her face. She wiped it away as she leaned up.

She lifted her new arm. It was scaled and had three joints and was quite a bit longer than her other.

It didn't matter.

She stepped off the table and felt his presence, and that choked everything else.

She fell off the table and crawled to the floor, but he reached down and put a finger to her chin.

He lifted her up and she came to her knees. He stared down until she rose to her feet.

He rubbed his coarse finger across her chin again as she looked him in the eyes.

"*You will not bow . . .*" he said with a whisper that was like nails across a chalkboard.

"Yes," she said, for what else could she do?

Their minds touched and she saw what he wanted:

The world and all within.

She understood this place better than he ever could. She could fight in a way he could not.

She could carry the war, and he could see to other business.

6

WHEN MILES ROLLED INTO BERLIN, he didn't precisely know how he and Kevin would be received, but he was ready for anything. He'd told Kevin as much too.

"Might give us a nod and send us on our way, or shoot us in the back of the head. Coin toss really."

Bullet in the back of the head? Slight nod and a gesture to the exit? Maybe it all depended on which asshole he made eye contact with.

Instead, the Soviets split the difference and locked them up in the most mediocre prison cell Miles had ever seen. In fact, he wasn't sure it had originally been a cell at all. It was a single room with carpet, albeit ugly carpet, and concrete walls.

"For the love of *God*," Miles said as he thumped his head against the only window they had. It wasn't even a particularly good window. Just a grimy plastic one Miles could barely see through. "Mate, if you sit on that toilet again, I'm going to scream until they shoot me."

Kevin huffed. "You think this was fun for me? There isn't even any toilet paper."

Miles leaned his head back and groaned loudly. "Give us a damn room where we can crack the window. And give this man some toilet paper. All I can think about is you walking around the room touching everything."

Kevin crouched down to a small bowl of water and dipped his hands in. "Hey at least they change the hand water once a day. Honestly, I'm surprised you've only used the toilet once. Or was it twice?"

"Listen, I'd prefer if you weren't keeping count. Is it safe to turn around?"

"Yep."

Miles glanced over his shoulder, cautious not to trust Kevin too much. "You know what pisses me off more than the toilet?"

"The window?"

"The window," Miles agreed. "But you know what else?"

"What?"

Miles gestured toward the floor. "Carpet. What kind of godless bastards put carpet in a jail cell."

Kevin winced and looked around. "I don't think it's a jail cell. I think this was like, uhh . . ." Kevin looked around. "Maybe an apartment?"

"You think the commies put ugly carpet down, a plastic window, concrete walls, and an open bathroom in an apartment?"

Kevin narrowed his eyes and kept looking. "*May*-be?"

"Yeah, maybe." Miles looked too. "Leave it to the Soviets to build an apartment that's nearly indistinguishable from a jail cell."

"*Well.*" Kevin rubbed his chin. "I think if it was a jail cell, there probably wouldn't be any carpet. Maybe everything else would be the same, but the carpet seems a little out of place."

"Doesn't it though?" Miles nodded. "I'm starting to lose count of how many days we've been here."

"Hmm." Kevin took a breath as he tried to think. "Well you used the toilet on the second day, so that means—"

Miles closed his eyes tight and shook his head. "Mate, what'd I say about keeping count? We're not going to start keeping track of time by how many times I've shit. That's *not* a thing we're going to do here.

I'm not going to spend my last few days talking about how many times I've had to squat with you in the room."

"You squat? I just sit down."

Miles held his hand up to silence Kevin. "We're done."

Kevin opened his mouth to speak but the lock on the door turned and a stone-faced soldier entered, a rifle slung over his shoulder.

"Here it is." Miles flashed a grim look to Kevin.

"Are you going to shoot us?" Kevin asked.

"No. I've been sent to retrieve you. You are the Americans?" the Soviet asked with a heavy accent.

"Fresh out of Americans, mate. I'm a Brit and this fellow is a kiwi."

"I'm not a kiwi *dick*, I'm an Australian."

"Same difference." Miles raised his shoulders.

Kevin hissed and shook his head.

The Soviet was unfazed. "The Grand Marshal wants to speak with you. Come with me."

Miles shared a look with Kevin and headed out.

They started down the hallway and the soldier walked behind them and directed them toward the stairs.

"What's this about? Any idea?" he said with a glance back to the soldier.

"You will speak with the Grand Marshal." He pointed Miles forward.

"Yeah, but is it like a *good* talk?" Kevin asked.

"Forward," the soldier ordered.

"English's not bad, mate." Miles flashed a look at him. "Did you—"

"*Forward.*"

Miles decided to shut up for the rest of the walk as the soldier led them out of the building and across the field, toward an old German military command center.

Miles had to squint from the sun, but he looked out to see civilians digging ditches, and CAG soldiers moving about. Helicopters were circling the area while jets flew past.

He nudged Kevin. "Looks like things aren't going too bad here."

The Soviet momentarily stepped in front of them and scanned his badge. The door rattled off something incomprehensible through a broken speaker. A moment later, there was a loud groan of metal on metal and the door finally slid aside.

The Soviet stepped aside and pointed. "Go."

They were led down a set of stairs and past guards in CAG into the command room.

Though the base was old, it was clear that new tactical and strategic command equipment had been set up. Some with bare wires running across the floor.

Seated officers with headsets spoke to soldiers in the field while green light from digital map screens glowed in front of them.

In the back of the room, one man was pointing at a digital overlay while others listened. He had a black synthetic skin weave jaw and his voice sounded like he chewed nails.

It was Grand Marshal Sergei Garin. Miles knew that without having ever seen the man before. The jaw was a dead giveaway, but it was the way the man carried himself that was the real kicker.

Miles' father would have said, *"He holds his chin like a man in charge."* Miles always wondered what the hell that meant, but looking at Garin, he understood.

That bastard held his chin like a man in charge.

Garin looked up when Miles and Kevin approached and the other officers turned their heads. Each of them came to focus on Miles and Kevin as they stopped in front of the table.

Miles felt an itch at the corner of his mouth, like he was supposed to introduce himself, but he wasn't sure why he was even here.

"I—uhh—I'm Miles Westwood, and this is my mate, Kevin—"

Garin interrupted when he reached back to grab something off a table: the notebooks Kevin had written in on the way to Berlin.

"Who wrote these?" Garin asked, the synthetics on his face making his voice almost a growl.

"He did." Miles thumbed at Kevin. He felt the weight of the officers' eyes on him.

"Yeah, I did." Kevin looked nervous, his eyes jumping as he looked at each of the men. "What we saw when we were out there."

"Out where?"

Kevin stuttered under Garin's gaze and Miles spoke up.

"Out *there*, mate."

"He's not your *mate*." A bald-headed officer growled at Miles.

Miles flashed a nervous smile. "We were in Moscow. Trekked our way over here. Been all up and down the continent, uhh—sir."

Garin looked to the bald officer and exchanged some words in Russian. Maybe it was exhaustion or stress, but Miles couldn't understand a word of it.

"What'd he say?" Kevin whispered, eliciting a look from Garin.

Miles grinned at Garin as he whispered back at Kevin. "*Mate*, he can hear you."

"Are they going to kill us?"

"No," Garin said. He set the journal down on the map screen and tapped it with a finger. "I only want to know if this is true."

"Truth as we know it ma—ehh—sir." Miles held up his hands. "Every word of it."

"These are reliable ways to detect the infiltrators?" the bald man asked.

"The what?" Miles frowned.

"The ones that look human. That enter into our cities." Garin shook the journals. "You have ways in here you say can detect which ones are enemies and which are not."

"Yeah, but . . ." Miles glanced between the men. "You didn't know that already?"

"We have not found any reliable method to detect them yet."

"You just make them get their bits out, mate." He let the word slip again before he quickly corrected it. "*Sir*."

Garin frowned and Miles wondered what was getting lost in translation.

"*Bits?*" Garin asked.

"Their uhh . . ." Miles gestured toward his crotch.

"Speak plainly, our translator is unavailable," the bald man said.

"Sorry to say, but you gotta have them get their cocks out. I saw them come out of the eggs, they don't have cocks or any nasty bits. It's all plain rubber down there. Smooth as a baby doll."

"No nipples or pubic hair either," Kevin said.

"Come on now," Miles frowned at him. "No need to get dirty here."

"Why are pubes worse than cocks?" Kevin asked.

"Now's not the time for debate." Miles sliced a hand through the air.

"Eggs?" Garin squinted his eyes as if the word confused him.

"Yeah, the eggs." Miles waited while a moment of silence passed.

"I don't think they know about the eggs," Kevin said.

"I know, I just—" Miles squeezed his eyes shut for a moment to clear his head and then held us his hand. "What *do* you know?"

Garin shook his head and the bald man crossed his arms.

Miles looked at Kevin and now he was the one to whisper.

"Fucking hell."

MILES STEPPED INTO THE BATHROOM, a plastic grin on his face. Somehow the muscles had locked in his face that way despite every Soviet looking stone faced or even bored. The grin stayed on his face as he walked toward the mirrors, but though he was walking calm and steady, his knees felt like they were about to shake.

They don't know anything.

That thought was rolling around Miles' head as he planted both hands on the sink and leaned forward.

He felt like he was going to gag. Instead, he looked up into the mirror.

His reflection grinned back at him, but his eyes told the truth. He could see that much.

He was ready to shit himself.

He'd just spent the last forty minutes smiling his ass off as he told Garin everything he knew of the monsters, but there were still more questions to come.

And Miles was the expert.

The weight of that responsibility had crawled up his back like a hairy spider with venom in its bite.

If Miles was an expert of anything, it was being able to bullshit.

But here he was, staring into the mirror and thinking that if he stopped grinning, his whole face might slide off.

"Get your shit together, mate," Miles said through clenched teeth. "You're an expert on the unnatural, aren't you? Well now you are for real."

Miles forced himself to lean up and take a breath. He still felt like panicking, but he'd learned long ago he was such a good liar, he could lie to himself. "You're fine. You're *fine*."

Now when his eyes popped open, the grin looked more sincere. He put two fingers out on both hands and massaged his face. The muscles were sore but as he massaged, the grin slipped off. "*You're* fine. *I'm* fine. Just gotta take a piss is all. That's all *you*—I—have to do." With a sigh, he flipped on the sink and splashed some water in his face. "Stop talking like a crazy person."

He walked over to the urinal, shaking out his arms and legs like he was getting ready for a sprint. He lined up and pulled his zipper down. He closed his eyes and leaned his head back.

He let the stream loose.

The door opened.

His stream sputtered as he heard steps come close.

"*Miles*," Kevin said. "Grand Marshal Garin had some thoughts."

"Sharing a toilet for a few days wasn't enough for you, mate? Give me a minute. It's a tad awkward having you at my back while I'm trying to drain the one-eyed snake." He let the stream go again.

"He said—"

"Fucking hell, Kevin." Miles shook it off and looked over his shoulder. "What did he say?"

"He said he's arranging a flight for us." Kevin grinned. "He's sending us to Washington."

"*What?*"

"There was an outbreak in New York."

Miles stared for a second, his dick still in his hand, but fortunately pointed in the right direction.

"He's going to send us to advise the president on the counter attack."

Miles froze in place.

Kevin frowned. "You okay?"

The plastic smile slid on once more. *"Fantastic, mate."*

7

ERKIN KAHN STEPPED into darkness as he descended the stairs of a half-destroyed building. Except for a single flood window, it was entirely dark.

The work here was nearly done. The cronux had overrun the city, and with the exception of a few holdouts, the fighting was over. He sent most of the horde out of the city, and now armed squads of Chinese soldiers patrolled the street with their CAG helmets blaring a single message in various languages.

"Do not leave your homes. Do not lock your doors. Those that disobey will be shot. Await further instructions."

Soon he would be done and a helicopter would arrive to move him, and the horde would follow.

But for now, he wanted time alone. A few creatures lingered behind him, but they were as much a part of him as his own hands.

He pressed the release button on his helmet, and it chirped as a dozen internal locks disconnected from his neck. He never got comfortable in the helmet. Even now, all he could manage to wear was a heavy chest piece and the helmet. The arms and legs had functions that were difficult to manage for new users, and he didn't have the time to train for it.

He dropped the helmet to the floor with a thud, and took a seat along a wall.

He rubbed his temple and closed his eyes.

Something strange was going on in his brain. It was like his mind was in mud, and each step was heavy and sluggish.

Just an hour ago, he was outside with the horde and he heard a young woman scream.

He hadn't seen her, but there was a snap within his brain, like the scream echoed inside.

"What?" he said to the empty room as he thought of the scream.

Creatures prowled into the room to take a place on the floor, like dogs at the feet of a master. A dead woman stumbled into the room, parasitic wisps squirming from an open wound on her neck.

Was she the one that screamed?

He could feel the parasites twisting around in her body as she thumped down to the floor. Her head rolled around like a ball on a rope, the dead and distant eyes falling on Erkin.

There was something familiar about the eyes . . .

He looked away and rubbed his temple again.

He was changing—his body was changing. He could feel the movement in his eyes, like tiny little worms crawling beneath the surface, and there was constant pressure within his guts—a throbbing he'd never experienced before.

Just two days ago, he'd collapsed to a knee in a hacking fit, and some medic ran over as he threw up two large bloated sacs of flesh.

Through it all, Erkin wasn't sure his pulse had even increased, but the medic had stared down at it with wide, fearful eyes.

"I think . . . I think those are your lungs."

If those were his lungs, then they'd become useless. He hadn't felt the need, nor desire, to breathe in some time, but he was still capable of speech.

That same medic told him that they intended to run extensive tests when they got him out of the field.

Yes, there was much to think about.

If they were his lungs, how had they even managed to get into his throat?

Had something pushed them there, like the squirming beneath his eyes?

It didn't matter.

It wasn't his eyes, his lungs, or even the crunch of bone as the creatures near him chewed on the meat they dragged in that concerned him.

No, it was the woman.

And her eyes.

And the scream.

A vision came over Erkin as he leaned forward to rest his elbows on his knees.

In his mind's eye, there was a house—one he'd forgotten—but he could see it now as clearly as he could see the woman.

And there, within his thoughts, he touched the walls of the house and heard a voice.

"Erkin."

It was the dead woman.

No. It was his wife.

He jolted up so suddenly, the cronux on the ground all shifted back in surprise.

His wife. They'd promised him his wife.

This had all been for her, and his daughter, for his family.

The fog shifted from his head.

"My wife," he said out loud. "Where is my wife?"

A flood broke inside him and his hand began to tremble.

The cronux all stirred with irritation.

He got to his feet and walked up the stairs, and the heads of the cronux twisted to follow him. Without command, they folded in behind him, following his lead.

Upstairs, light shone through the windows and the open door. Erkin felt an urgency that nearly made him stumble as he stepped out onto the streets. A squad of soldiers marched past him, their loudspeakers booming through their head mics.

Erkin had to put his hands on his ears as they went past.

"*Where is my wife?*" he said again, as if afraid to forget her once more.

He glanced either way down the streets looking for the command crew.

Instead, he saw a small flash of light in the distance on a rooftop.

It was the glint of a rifle scope.

And it was only in that moment, as he heard the crack of the shot, that he realized he'd left his helmet back on the floor.

The blast rocked his head back, and Erkin saw his own brains splash against the wall.

As the darkness swallowed him, he saw the cronux rush past, swarming the Chinese squad and everything else in a fit of madness.

A BULLET IN THE BRAIN.

A small piece of metal.

That was all it took for the ground to shift beneath Zhao's feet.

If plans were empires, then Zhao's were crumbling before his eyes.

He'd been in a meeting discussing the new trade terms within the South Asian Alliance when his secretary leaned down and whispered into his ear.

"*Sir, the Dragon has been shot.*"

Zhao had felt his blood run cold.

"*But he still lives.*"

Oh, the tides of fate were cruel. How foolish had Zhao been to build his vision on the back of one man?

He ended the meeting at that very moment and summoned Wu.

That had been two days ago.

Now the two were sitting in Zhao's office, a large screen on the wall displayed the Dragon's open brain and a surgeon's hands working to rewire it.

The surgeon, Dr. Feng, was a renowned brain and cybernetics specialist in Beijing.

Zhao's own personal transport had flown him north to the hospital.

A lit cigarette hung from Wu's lips as they both watched the surgery. No one else dared to slouch in front of Zhao, but there was Wu, lounging in his chair with a lit cigarette as the fate of China unfolded before them.

It was as if the man enjoyed pushing his limits with Zhao.

Wu pulled the cigarette from his mouth. Smoke snaked out as he spoke. "The sniper was a woman. Her brothers were rounded up, but she passed the initial inspection. My, what awful work a single woman with a rifle can do."

"Has she been apprehended?" Zhao asked, not taking his eyes from the screen.

"Killed in a shootout." Wu smothered the cigarette in an ashtray. "An unfortunate turn of events, as I would have preferred a slower end. I've ordered that all men, women, and children be detained. Simply tell us how many dead bodies would pay the girl's debt and we'll see to it."

"In time. Let us focus on the future." Zhao never took his eyes from the surgery. "Soon the demons will arrive at the gates of China once more."

"The Dragon's horde is stable in Mongolia." Wu lifted a shoulder. "So long as none approach too closely. There was an apparent accident and a squad of our soldiers were lost, but they know better now. There is the occasional drifter, but we try to contain and dispatch any that stray far from the group."

"Then we must believe there is something still in the Dragon that holds the horde in place. But we've already seen small groups of the creatures arriving from the Soviet Union."

"Scouts, testing the field before an invasion. Either way, it'll make the governors nervous."

"Indeed."

"Our Dragon has killed one god. He will kill another. Professor Ghao has assured me that the Dragonskin program will produce another success soon."

"May I speak freely, Chairman?" Wu crossed his legs and put his hands on his armrests.

Zhao spared him a look. "The only reason I accept your disrespect is because you are one of the few who will."

"I've seen the data and Ghao is no closer to another Dragon than she was a month ago. She'll say whatever she believes you'd like to hear."

Zhao took a deep breath. Fear among his subordinates was instrumental for structure and control, but it had its disadvantages. "Then you will go and see for yourself. Tell me what we can do to improve the Professor Ghao's progress."

"As I said, I've looked at the numbers. We must increase the rate of experimentation, it's becoming hard to gather volunteers. We've depleted many of the shelters, orphanages, camps, and prisons. I suggest we honor the populace by including them in the program."

"We will do as we must. Gather those that you need."

Wu tipped his head.

Zhao turned to stare Wu in the eyes. "We can no longer build our destiny upon the back of a single Dragon, not when he appears so fragile."

"About that . . ." Wu's cigarette smoldered, sending curls of smoke into the air. "There is research from the North Japanese that I believe would be useful to use. We were able to retrieve many of the Japanese specialists as their capital fell, and I believe their insight could be useful to our own specialists."

"Speak plainly."

"The Japanese have found ways to further augment our bodies beyond simple mechanized replacement limbs." Wu gestured toward the screen where the surgeon's hands worked to remove a shattered piece of the bullet from the brain. "The Dragon is a unique being with a unique purpose. Now that he's opened up, why should we put him back together the way he was when there are so many other wonderful things we could gift him? The North Japanese have accomplished many impressive things and I'm told our options are truly wide and considerable."

Zhao looked back to the surgery. Bright red blood ran down the grooves of the brain.

"We will do as we must. For the glory of the People's Republic."

Wu settled back into his seat, and echoed the words.

"For the glory of the People's Republic."

8

In a small, darkly lit room, the heads of Washington sat around a table smoking cigars.

John Winters wasn't there.

There were fewer of them than there had been. That same wave of assassinations that propelled the career of John Winters culled their numbers.

And it also provided opportunities for those with ambition.

The U.S. Senate majority leader, Tom McIntyre, was in one corner of the table, a fat cigar stuck between his lips.

A few years back, an artery in his brain collapsed—or as McIntyre put it, *popped*—and led to a massive stroke. If not for the miracle of modern medicine, and a yard or so of synthetic vein cable, Tom McIntyre would be dead.

But he was not.

Instead, he was in a dimly lit room, a lit cigar between his lips, discussing the future of the country.

The future of John Winters.

But at the moment, he was simply listening.

"The way I see it, a bullet in the head would be too nice," Senator Garnett said, pointing his sausage of a finger at the table. He sneered, and every roll on his neck jiggled. "I'll never forgive the son of a bitch for how he rolled over for the Russians, after what they did to us. The bastards were down. One good stomp on the back of their head was all it'd taken."

Senator Linda Hayward, the newly elected Speaker of the House of Representatives, shook her head. "He did what he had to do then. We couldn't have a nuclear war. But this business with New York, sealing them off? He's a coward. Civilians are stuck behind the line while he drags his feet on a military counterattack. I'd like it if he had the same zeal for New York as he did with his reelection campaigns."

Senator Gregan, House whip, shook his head. "I'm with Garnett. The bastards killed our *goddamn* president. It's unforgivable. We should have turned half the continent into glass and taken care of two problems at once. If we did that, there wouldn't even *be* a problem in New York."

Others in the small room began to speak, and McIntyre took the moment to blink, something he had to remind himself to do on occasion ever since the vein popped. When he waited too long, his eyelids felt like they were rubbing sandpaper over his eyes, so he had to do it slowly.

McIntyre leaned in toward the table and pulled the cigar out, blowing a wave of smoke. "Maybe he's a traitor, or maybe he's a pussy. Here's what *is* important. He's in charge."

Senator Garnett huffed at that, his flesh jiggling. "And we've agreed that's a problem because the bastard won't listen."

McIntyre held up a finger to the senator, and then counted off fingers. "One. After that wave of resignations, John has only half his cabinet filled and no vice president. If he's deposed, then leadership falls to you, Speaker." He pointed at her and then held up another finger. "Two. With the public distracted by New York, there might be room for a change of leadership. And three, there's a tightening window for when we can act. As soon as he has a full team and has courted off a few distractions, he'll be much harder to deal with."

Gregan shook his head. "That's on you McIntyre, are you going to let the Senate approve his people?"

McIntyre grunted. "Oh, you think it'd play well for my political fortunes if we blue balled his staff in the middle of a *goddamn* alien invasion? I'll have to play ball if it comes to that, so we better move fast."

Garnett frowned. "What do you want then? No way to impeach fast, not with those few hapless bastards in the Senate. It'll drag on for months, and it'll fail anyway."

McIntyre blinked. "I don't want to impeach him. I'm suggesting we authorize the McCarthy clause."

Garnett raised his eyebrows. "The McCarthy clause? You want to say he's working for the Soviets?"

"Said it yourself, didn't you? He bent over for them when they asked. We'll present the evidence to the council and ask for a stay of leadership while we investigate. Without a vice president, that'll trigger your accession, Speaker."

Garnett snapped his thumbs. "You're an evil bastard, McIntyre, but it'll work."

"Oh, I know it will." He plugged the cigar back into his mouth. "Wouldn't have said it otherwise."

Hayward tipped her head back. "McCarthy clause isn't that cut and dry. This'll put blood on the table. Things will get nasty."

McIntyre blinked again, and he could practically hear the grind on his dry eyeballs as he asked, "So you're not interested?"

"I didn't say that." She leaned back in her seat.

"I like the sound of *Ms. President*."

* * *

JOHN WINTERS STARED AT A SCREEN. He put the vid on mute. It was bad enough to look at what was happening, he didn't want to hear it.

He couldn't understand what was being said anyway.

On the vid, a man with a red bandana over his mouth thrust a finger at the camera and moved as if he were shouting. He pointed over at lines of soldiers in camouflage, blindfolded and on their knees.

The man with the red bandana gestured to someone off screen and they handed him a pistol. He turned and aimed at one of the kneeling men and blew his brains out.

He then started down the line, and though it was muted, John could hear the sound in his brain each time.

Bang.

Bang.

Bang.

"That's enough, Jim." John held up his hand.

The vid screen flipped and now the American ambassador to Venezuela, Jim Baker, a disheveled looking man in a suit, but with the tie deeply loosened. Static buzzed across the vidfeed.

"Things are getting out of hand here," the ambassador said. *"The peace accords are shattered and there are so many sides in this conflict I can't keep count. A militia from Brazil was here yesterday, but Venezuelan forces put them out. I'm hearing rumors that Colombian Special Forces are conducting airdrops in the jungles and putting up IEDs to kill farmers and travelers."*

"Christ Almighty." John ground his teeth and shook his head. "Have you prepared for evacuation?"

The ambassador sighed deeply. *"They've all steered clear of the embassy, and we've gathered supplies for an extended lockdown. Our defense forces are also prepared."*

"What are you saying then?"

"I'm saying I spent fifteen years helping construct the peace accords, and I'm unwilling to back out now. But I will evacuate nonessential staff and our families."

"Jim, I'll let you make the call, but I want you to know that insurgent forces in North Japan killed a squad of South Japanese, and they responded by executing a dozen or so villagers. I've lost touch with the ambassador to Morocco after he reported a cronux breakout. China has annexed a portion of Mongolia and all the neighboring countries have contacted us for aid against threats to their sovereignty. And we've yet to contain the spread in New York. If you don't leave now, we might not be able to get you later."

Jim Baker listened with glass-like eyes, and nodded his head. *"I understand the circumstances, sir. I wish to stay, but I'll give the choice to all staff."*

"God be with you Jim. You're one of the good ones," he said before signing out of the call.

John's secretary tapped on the door and stuck her head in. "Sir, your finance minister is here."

"Send him in." John leaned back in his chair and grabbed a glass of water. His hand was shaking. Either it was a lack of sleep, a lack of food, or just his nerves—God only knew what anymore. He gulped down the water and then laced his fingers together. That kept them from shaking.

The finance minister, William Turner, entered, but before he'd even sat down, John spoke.

"What's your report on the European bailout? They send me desperate messages every day."

William shook his head. "Impossible. The U.S. dollar's inflation has hit a fifty-year high. With our foreign partners diminishing or halting their exports, our supply lines are nonexistent. It doesn't matter how much money you have, there simply isn't anything to spend it on."

John nodded his head. "I understand. Is Australia still maintaining their exports?"

"Yes, but it's slowed. They're not gathering the raw materials from Africa and Asia anymore for most of their goods, and their courts have put on injunctions to keep critical exports within the country."

"Such as?"

"The few raw materials they do have: iron ore, oil, copper, and several others. They've also put a stay on beef, rice, medical supplies, and munitions."

"The Japanese import most of their food from the Australians. Connect with our team there and see if we can improve negotiations. Tell the Australians we'll see to it that our trade with them keeps flowing so long as they keep outsourcing to the countries that need it."

"I'll try, but they're scared, Mr. President."

John scoffed. "We're all scared, but how long will it take for the cronux to spread to Australia if the Japanese starve, or if Africa runs out of medical supplies?"

"I'll see what I can do," William said, and John dismissed him with a nod of his head.

As soon as the door closed, John hit a button on the call line on his desk. "Put me through to Roles."

"Right away sir," the secretary responded.

John let go of the call button and grabbed a pen. It had been a while since he'd done anything more than scribble a few notes, but nothing was secure these days. He barely trusted his computer anymore.

He wrote out a series of notes until his secretary's voice rang over the call line again.

"Sir, I have Secretary Roles connected."

"Put him through."

The vid screen in front of John lit up and Roles was there, his hands folded in front of him. *"Yes, Mr. President?"* he said.

"Roles, I need an update on the Chinese situation."

"Their Dragonskin program is ramping up activity. We've seen an increase in people going in. As far as my agents can tell, they're just snatching people off the street now and incinerating the bodies."

"There haven't been any more successes?"

"Not that I'm aware of, but there could be. I haven't gotten eyes inside the facility yet."

"And what about reports of their agent being shot, is he dead?"

"No. They've moved him back in country to perform surgery. My agent inside told me she believes he'll live, but it's anyone's guess how functional he'll be. The horde hasn't moved from Mongolia, but my agent reports that there have been some that have broken away and headed to the Dragon. It appears like he has some kind of subconscious control over them, but I'm really only speculating."

"They're allowing cronux to enter the city?"

"No. They've shot any that have tried. But each day, more break from the horde and head that way."

"I see. Whole world is falling apart, and my brain feels like it's going to leak out of my head. The Senate is slow-walking my proposed cabinet, so all the new appointees are in an acting position. With McAndrews gone, I'm hardly able to delegate any decisions, or even locate any more suitable staff."

Roles only nodded, his whole body barely moving.

John squeezed his own hands together before pulling them apart. This time they didn't shake.

"What'd you do with his McAndrews' body?" John asked.

Ever the professional, Roles had only a hint of a frown. *"Come again sir?"*

"I said what did you do with the body?"

"Frankly sir, I don't know what you're getting at."

John leaned back from the screen and waved a hand over a desk sensor. There was a click as an embedded computer rose up from the wood. John hit a few buttons and a report was sent to Roles.

Though Roles could see the report, John could only see his face. He watched carefully as Roles went over the report.

Roles exhaled and shook his head as if he were still unsure.

"Those are details the FBI has uncovered of communications between McAndrews with both the Chinese and the Soviets. But they weren't the only ones looking at the reports. There was another computer signal that signed in to view them. The FBI doesn't know who it belongs to, but I've seen it before. It was used to look over Alice's files when they were still classified and out of your reach, Roles. That's your signal. You killed McAndrews." John held the man's stare for a moment before speaking. "Where's the body?"

Roles held still. A moment of silence passed between them.

"Gone," Roles finally said. *"But since I haven't answered a knock from the FBI, I have to assume you're either waiting for my resignation or you have other ideas."*

"Other ideas. Yeah." John spoke in a firm voice. "Do you know who the NAS are?"

Roles nodded. *"New American Sons. A violent secessionist group."*

"They've been building a small community of people that say that cronux aren't real, that it's all just a power grab. But that's all they were doing until just two hours ago. They attacked a government installation and a few people are dead. They're trying to spark a civil war. The point is, I have more problems than I have hands to solve them. You're an evil bastard, Roles, but one of the few competent people I have around me. And I believe under all those sins, you're still a patriot, and these are uncertain times."

Roles nodded, but was otherwise silent.

John pointed a finger at the screen. "Don't go around killing anyone else without speaking to me first."

"I understand."

"Good." He let out a breath and took a drink of water. "Because I sure as hell don't need any more distractions."

9

MARAT WAS NERVOUS, but he was always nervous.

That's why he smoked so much.

He barely saw Moller anymore, and that meant he had to venture out on his own to get cigarettes. He felt like there were always eyes on him when he moved through the base. It wouldn't surprise him at all to turn a corner only to get met with a kick in the balls, or worse, a bullet in the face.

Though he had his own room, he had to adhere to some parts of the strange agreements he'd made with the base chief.

Like eating in the chow hall with the military men.

He'd limit himself to eating there once a day or so, and he'd just pack his pockets with crackers and ketchup to eat back in his room.

One can only do so many days of stale cracker bags and squeezed ketchup packets, though, and Marat dared an attempt at breakfast.

With his head down and glancing back and forth like he was afraid his mom would find him with a titty magazine, he sat down at a table.

Not two bites into it, and an enlisted man sat down across from him.

"My father was killed by communist."

Hell of a way to begin a conversation.

Marat had the sudden urge to say, *"Eat shit fat beef."* But that had never worked before. Instead he felt a tug in his gut, and he feigned a smile and said, *"Such a coincidence. Mine was too."*

The man cracked a smile and laughed. Why though, Marat wasn't sure. Was that some kind of dark humor that Americans enjoyed or were they simply an odd and undecipherable people?

He'd been out again and a man glared at him. Marat smiled and said the first thing he thought of, *"My father was killed by communist."*

The man frowned, and then Marat just felt like an asshole.

He knew those words weren't magic. They just popped out like it was natural instinct for him to look like an idiot.

But even when he tried conversation starters he read from his grammar and conversation book, it still never went well.

"How is the weather?" he asked a man yesterday as they both walked outside.

The guy looked around as if it was obvious. "It's cloudy."

Oh, Marat had fucked it up. *"No, no, no, I mean you enjoy the weather?"* he said in a desperate attempt to correct the mistake.

"Do I enjoy cloudy weather? No. I don't." The man was still confused and took Marat's moment of pause to walk away.

The grammar and conversation book always had a back and forth conversation. It was practically mathematical. Had Marat really messed it all up, or had that guy? The man was *supposed* to respond and then ask Marat how he felt about the weather.

So either the book was full of shit, or maybe it was Marat's accent. He sounded like an idiot despite the fact his IQ was twice as high as any idiot giving him side eyes here.

So long as he sounded like an unstable moron, he was either going to be laughed at or dismissed . . . and that might mean the best shot he had at a love life would be the Americans' abundant supply of porn.

That inspired Marat to try just a *little* harder. Not the porn, but the idea that even if he did find himself in a conversation with a Hollywood blonde, she'd likely be confused at his attempts to hit on her, or simply laugh at his accent.

So now, he was in his room with the shades drawn, his back

arched as he leaned forward with his elbows on his knees and a cigarette in his mouth. He listened to the smooth feminine voice coming from a small audio device on his desk.

"The cow jumps over the fence, so the farmer frowns."

Marat pulled his cigarette from his mouth and rolled it up and down between his two fingers. He took a breath and tried his best to repeat the phrase.

"The cow—"

The device flashed red, his accent was too thick. Marat twisted his head back with irritation.

The device spoke again, the voice irritatingly calm and patient.

"The cow jumps over the fence, so the farmer frowns."

This was humiliating. Marat had such a gifted mind that he was drafted into Soviet research and development before he'd even finished his degree. He was put into a program that made contact with aliens, and here he was sounding like a moron to every American whenever he opened up his mouth because he couldn't pronounce words like *the* correctly.

He'd humbled himself, and on their last visit, he asked Moller to order him a language assistant device to help improve his pronunciation, but he was still stuck on the elementary level.

"The cow jumps over the fence, so the farmer frowns," it repeated.

Marat took a deep breath and let his shoulders relax.

"The cow—"

It flashed red again.

He turned and kicked his desk hard. This was what his life was now. Not studying computer science or working on the razor's edge of the tech field, no, no, no, he was here getting pissed off at a school device for children.

"The cow jumps—"

"I know, I know!" he shouted at it and held up a hand.

He pinched his nose and closed his eyes tight—his cigarette smoldered in the dark.

His eyes popped open and he let out a breath.

"The cow—"

It flashed red.

"You fucker!" he yelled and jumped out of the seat. He pointed at it and cursed in both Russian and Ukrainian as the device continually flashed red with the last flash as green.

Marat put his hands up and bent down to yell at the device's green light. *"You fucking lie!"*

"The cow jumps—"

"I know, I know." He rolled his hand and stiffened his back. He tilted his head up and took a puff of his cigarette. He exhaled and stared at the ceiling.

"The cow jumps over the fence, so the farmer frowns," he finished and glanced down.

The light was yellow.

Marat made a face, but decided he'd accept it. He could live with yellow. He'd heard American women enjoyed British accents. Perhaps his would be the same? He was trying his best to fit in, but it was hard. He walked over to the window and pulled the shade open. He peeked out. Everything was so spacious. It was sickening. It made him feel exposed, like he'd forgotten to wear his pants. He much preferred a nice thick crowd, pick pockets and all.

Marat plugged the cigarette between his lips and rubbed his temples with both hands. He pulled down on his face, stretching his eyes open, and moaned from exhaustion.

There was a knock at his door that made him jump and the cigarette fell out of his mouth.

"Shit!" he said as he grabbed it and smashed his foot where it fell.

There was another knock. *"Marat, it's me. We've got work to do."*

Moller. In an instant, Marat felt the butterflies flutter in his stomach. He'd mostly given up on any hopes of that—she certainly didn't seem interested at all.

She knocked again. *"Marat? Open the door."*

Marat cleared his throat and tried his best to focus his English. "A minute." He glanced down at his bare legs and then around his cluttered room. "I need to find pants."

MARAT STOOD NEXT TO A JEEP, his arm resting on the hood as he watched the Soviet plane descend onto the private Washington airstrip. A squad of airmen in camouflage stood with him.

He imagined it was a tense moment for everyone. Watching an airplane from the Soviet Union land on their airstrip with a couple of experts on the cronux invasion.

Their nerves must all be on end.

But Marat? He was having trouble keeping his eyes off of Moller.

She'd cruelly decided to stand in front of him, and her hair was fastened up in a ponytail. He could see her neck.

My God, how he could see her neck.

He hadn't known it until this moment, but now he did.

He was really into necks, he just never realized it, or knew if it was even a thing at all.

"What are you thinking, commie?" a man to his right said, a pinch of tobacco under his lip. "Hoping a few of your friends come out?" He spit by Marat's feet.

Marat wasn't sure how to respond, so he went with the first thing that came to mind. "My father was killed by communist."

"Say what now?" The man's face tightened with confusion.

The officer at the jeep shot a look at the man and tipped his chin toward the plane. "Cut the shit, those aren't even Soviets. It's some washed-up TV host."

"Could be a trick," the private said.

"If it is, it'd be a dumb one," Moller said and watched the plane come to a halt.

Marat barely noticed, he was too busy wondering why the man had seemed confused. Was it his accent?

The cow jumps over the fence, so the farmer frowns. Marat mumbled under his breath.

A standby crew drove up in a small truck and a man jumped out to direct the plane. When it came to a halt, the door opened and stairs extended.

Marat stopped mumbling and watched carefully. Though the man arriving was some kind of TV star, Marat had of course never seen any of his shows. And as the doors to the plane opened, Marat expected some kind of devilishly handsome man with a smile that could melt a young woman's heart.

Instead, a haggard man with his hand up to block the glaring sun stepped out of the plane, and another man with wide, tired eyes followed him.

The officer must have had similar disappointed feelings. *"Hope this isn't a waste of time,"* he mumbled, and strolled forward. *"Mr. Westwood,"* he called out loud enough to be heard over the engine of the plane. *"Welcome to Washington."*

Miles grinned as he moved over and offered his hand. "Thank you. Now where the hell can I get a hamburger? The damn Soviets don't have anything that doesn't taste like sawdust."

MILES YAWNED and looked around the cold, sterile, white room.

"Why the hell does it seem like we keep getting moved from one prison room to the next?"

Kevin leaned onto the table with his head in his hands. "Because we keep getting moved from one prison room to the next."

Miles stood up and started to pace the room. "Now see, the Soviets putting our arses on lock down was sound logic, but the Americans too?" He glared up at a camera in the corner of the room and made an obvious and exaggerated scratch at his crotch.

It was just then that the door opened and the blonde agent that had introduced herself as *Lacey Moller* entered, followed by a thin gangly man.

Miles fanned his arms out. "How lovely to see you again."

"I'm sorry, we had some things to attend to before coming," Moller said as she found a seat.

"Fancy that." Miles took a seat at the table. "Who's he?"

.Z. FOSTER

Moller placed a datapad on the table. "Marat Ivanov, he worked on the gate in Moscow."

Kevin perked up. "He did?"

Marat flashed a look at them before turning his eyes away.

She nodded. "He was there when they made first contact."

"Bit young for R&D, aren't you?" Miles asked.

"The Soviet Union drafted him into service before he'd finished college. He's a genius," Moller said.

Marat gave an unpleasant smile but still looked away.

Kevin pointed at his chest. "I got a video from inside the facility. I saw what you were doing."

"That's the truth of it," Miles said. "That little video was what sparked our whole little galavant across the Soviet Union."

Marat looked up, and spoke with a heavy accent, "You did? From who?"

Kevin shook his head. "Anonymous source."

Marat frowned and settled back into his seat.

Miles shook his head. "Don't know who it was from, but it was all peaches. Whoever it was is dead now, I'm sure. At any rate, all cards on the table, Moller, I'm not precisely sure what it is my mate and I are doing here with you and Mr. Ivanov here. Kevin and I know a *wee bit* about what's going on, but that's about it."

Moller pressed a button on her datapad. A document lit up and she used her finger to scroll through it for a few moments. "The Soviets sent over a report but it's a bit scarce on details. It says you survived in the field and encountered several entities. You also learned how to detect the Sleepers."

"That's what you call them?" Miles shrugged his shoulders.

"What do you call them?" she asked.

"Chimera," Kevin answered.

"Is that what *we* call them?" Miles shrugged. "News to me."

Kevin nodded. "I don't know. It's what I keep coming up with when I think of them. Chimera, like the Greek monster."

"Works for me." Moller gave a flat smile.

Miles went on, "They're easy enough to detect. No nasty bits on them. It's all in the report." He pointed at her datapad.

"How'd you survive in the field with no weapons or armor?" she asked.

Kevin snorted. "Do you know who he is?"

"Kevin, come on mate." Miles waved him down.

"Have you ever seen his show? He's been in and out of dangerous situations before."

"Easy, *easy*." Miles flashed an awkward grin at Moller.

"I know who he is, and I know how dangerous the situation in the Soviet Union is," Moller said.

"Here's the thing of it. We moved cautiously. We observed, and we planned what we did," Miles said.

"And you saved people. A whole convoy by the report." Moller slid the datapad aside and folded her hands together. "Here it is then, Miles, *all cards on the table*. We four are the leading experts on the cronux and you're here to help form the American defensive strategy. Marat here is an expert on the gates, you two are experts on field strategy, and I've survived more combat encounters with them than any other person alive. I'm afraid we don't have long, because I'll have to leave tomorrow. I have to go up North and observe the situation with New York, so we better get to work right away before you meet him."

"Meet who?"

"John Winters, president of the United States."

10

OLD IN THE ways of war but young in flesh, the Janissary was born again. With the help of his acolytes, he left his old body—now a dried husk. A dark ritual moved his essence fully into the hive mind.

He drifted there for a time as a being with no body, or understanding of the world. He floated in the inky dark pool of the hive mind, no ability to form conscious thought or reason.

But he came out of it now, screaming, for the hive mind was a horrible place to live even for one like him.

With a three-fingered hand, he broke through the crust of an egg, and he moaned, for the pain was terrible. His new body was wet and steaming as he crawled out. He tore the fleshy egg and spilled the liquid stew onto the floor, as the air needled his fresh skin, making his body tighten.

All around him, long-legged cronux crouched and waited in silence as the Janissary took form again.

He scratched a hand across his face and pulled back excess skin and slung it away. He opened his new eyes for the first time.

Those around him, his brothers, his followers, all watched him with black glassy eyes.

This horde was not the same as before.

This was a new breed altogether.

His old coven had given their lives for the transfer, but new servants were born, and now, with the rebirth of the Janissary, a new coven was formed.

The Janissary rose to his feet, a tail snaking behind him. And though his frame was now something humanlike, he still stood massively tall in comparison.

He opened his mouth and spewed out fluid.

Now, with a breath of air, he tilted his head back and moved to the window, where rays of light were cutting through.

He saw the sun shining down upon the city, along with jets screaming above and dropping explosives upon the horde. Black smoke choked the sky while buildings burned and others collapsed sending dust clouds into the air. The Janissary could feel the horde moving through the city, pushing through the enemy's defenses.

They were strong, but they were mindless and unorganized.

That would change now with his presence.

"Ah—" the Janissary growled the word, and scar tissue bubbled up his throat. He spit it out, and took a breath to speak the word more clearly. "Ah-mer-i-ca."

PHILIP VOLMAR MADE the worst decision of his life when he turned eighteen. It was right after a spat with his mother when she'd caught him pants down with his girlfriend in his room again.

"I told you, none of that in my house!"

Philip thought he'd show her what he thought about *her house* and he went down to the local recruitment center and signed the dotted line for the U.S. Army. That pissed her off. He was sure he had a smile a mile wide when he showed her the papers. Looking back now, it seems like an odd way to teach his mom a lesson on leaving him alone with his girlfriend, because as it turns out, the Army's not too keen on giving you time to bang your girlfriend either.

A few months later, he was still in the Army, but his girlfriend was a fading memory. But hell, that was life right?

Still, things weren't all bad. Sure, it was a real kick in the balls when it all started, but it did put a little discipline in his life, not to mention Philip—or rather, Volmar now that he was in the military—hadn't really had any career aspirations.

He'd made up with his mom later and decided to make the most of things. He'd hang tough and get the benefits that came with service, and maybe find some gig when he got out. He deployed overseas, but even then he'd been lucky enough to not get into anything dirty.

All said and done, things weren't going too bad.

Until the fucking aliens invaded.

Of course, Volmar had been hearing the reports of them spreading through the Soviet Union, but honest to God, you never knew what the hell you could trust coming out of there. One of his fellow grunts had said as much too.

"Know what I think? It's all bullshit. The Soviets are collapsing, and they're going to start calling it 'aliens' to justify massive use of force. Do those goddamn Russians really think we're that stupid?"

Oh yeah. Those stupid bastards. Real dumb shits thinking they could trick everyone into believing aliens were really coming.

But then there were videos, but hell, a kid with a computer in his room could make a video.

Volmar had even been on some of the message boards with the New American Sons where they talked about how the U.S. government was going to get in on it so they could start justifying a further clampdown on freedoms here.

Volmar wasn't sure how he felt about it. The news sounded convincing, but so did everyone saying it was bullshit; aliens with no eyes but plenty of teeth, hadn't he seen that movie before?

It all sounded like fantasy really.

That was until they landed in New York.

Oh, he was certain they were real now.

He'd been killing them for days.

Piled up behind a makeshift barrier of broken cars and whatever the hell else was laying out, his unit had been holding the flood of ugly nightmares back on a single large street while evacuations were conducted in New York. The unfortunate location of New York meant that every exit out of there was a god-awful choke point. Supposedly cars ended up colliding on the bridge bringing everything to a standstill and the U.S. Army just rolled in there and started knocking shit off the bridge and into the water to make way for more refugees.

He'd have loved to have been there, rolling around in a tank, or wearing some mechanized lift enhancements to throw cars off a bridge.

But no. He signed the dotted line for infantry.

So no car throwin' for him.

He manned the wall.

And the awful things seemed to try to run them over every few hours.

They were dumb as hell; they'd just come rolling in from a distance, so many packed together you couldn't tell one from the another, and they'd scream like their skin was on fire. Oddly enough, sometimes their skin was on fire but they seemed totally indifferent to that.

They were dumb all right, but they'd nearly broken over Volmar's barrier several times, and military was spread so thin now they weren't getting relieved.

It was exhausting.

He really needed a kick.

Volmar sat down on his ass and held out an open hand. "Give me a jack, I'm about to shit out my eyebrows."

Two-ton, the fattest son of a bitch in the unit, shifted toward Volmar. "The hell does that mean?"

"I don't know man, I'm tired." Volmar shook his hand to speed Two-ton up.

Two-ton dug a stim out of his pack and slapped it into Volmar's hand.

Volmar flattened his back against the broken car barrier and sat his rifle in his lap. He pressed a release on his CAG sleeve, and a notch with a small port lifted up on the armor. He jacked the stim in and felt the liquid lightning roll over him. He took a breath and tossed the empty container away. "If I have to do any more stims, I really will shit out my eyebrows."

"When the hell are we getting relieved?" Two-ton said as he turned his attention back to the road.

"Who knows." Volmar looked over the barrier. There was a near-endless pile of dead bodies. So much so, that it was starting to create a barrier of its own. The sergeant threw out a heat frag a few hours ago to cake it all down, and by God was Volmar glad he had a CAG helmet, because that smell must have been horrendous.

Hold the line while units do search and rescue. That was the job. Apparently they were still dragging civis out, and Volmar was just glad he didn't have that job. Given the choice, he'd rather be flipping cars; but if the options were search and rescue or manning the wall, then there really was no choice at all. The wall wasn't a cake walk, but manning the defenses here was prime versus going in there and looking for people who were almost certainly dead.

So long as those dumb bastards kept coming up front and center, Volmar was certain there wouldn't be a—

There was movement in the distance.

"Volmar, do you have eyes on it?" a voice buzzed through the helmet speakers.

"Confirmed," Volmar answered, "but I can't make a damn thing out."

"Just one from your vantage point?"

"Confirmed. Best I can tell."

"Keep on it."

"Confirmed." Volmar glanced back. His squad had taken up various points in nearby buildings, but the smoke and chemicals in the air did make the little details hard from high up.

He looked forward again and put his finger to a dial wheel on his helmet. He rotated it and heard a *click-click-click* as the lenses magnified.

It was a woman, beat to hell and back by the looks of it, but one could expect that from a single person leaving an alien-infested war zone. She had a long blanket or something wrapped around her and over her head, holding it tight across her stomach.

She stumbled over the bodies and Volmar couldn't help but wince. He saw her tumble a few times, but she kept that blanket tight against her.

Volmar thought she was probably wounded, but an anxious feeling rolled over him.

What if she has a baby there?

"*Fuck*," he hissed and leaned up from the barrier. "Hey! *Hey!* Over here! Get over here, quick!"

He saw her take a step and one foot slid on a half-melted body, the charred skin giving way.

Volmar grunted and shook his head. Disgusting.

He pressed the call button on his helmet. "Corporal, it appears to be a civi. Can I jump the wall and go retrieve?"

"*Negative, hold position.*"

"Confirmed." Volmar clicked off the call. "Dick."

"No kidding," Two-ton said.

The woman kept stumbling through the bodies and shaking.

"How the hell do you think someone like that even survives out there?" Two-ton asked.

"Hell if I know." Volmar waved her over. "Come on, you're almost here."

She hurried now, seemingly trying to step between the bodies onto the bare pavement, but there was only so much of that.

She got close enough that Volmar could see her face. An old woman with deep wrinkles.

He handed his rifle to Two-ton and took a step up to reach for her.

She reached out with one hand, but kept the blanket pinned with the other.

"Give me your other hand," Volmar said, but she didn't offer it, she only pulled with the one. "Well all right then." He squeezed around one hand and used his other to grab her elbow. He pulled her over the barrier.

Two-ton helped her to the ground. "Hell lady, how long have you been crawling out there?"

"*It's a rainy day,*" she said with a hoarse voice.

Volmar looked up, but there wasn't any rain.

"You need some water?" he asked.

"*It's a rainy day.*" Her cold eyes met Volmar's, and he stopped in his tracks.

"Not a drop, lady," Two-ton said. "You're safe now though, you stay with us until we can get a team to swing by and get you."

Volmar felt an itch crawl up his back. "Here." He gestured toward Two-ton and the man handed Volmar his rifle back.

Volmar turned off his external speakers so the woman wouldn't hear him and opened up another call.

"Corporal, we've got her here, but she's out of it."

"*What do you mean?*"

"I mean she's insane."

"*It's a rainy day,*" the woman spouted again.

Volmar flashed a look toward her. "Keeps talking about rain and I sure as hell haven't felt a drop."

"*Stash her somewhere out of the way until transport arrives.*"

"Confirmed."

Another voice came on the line. "*We've got movement sir.*"

"*Another wave?*" the Corporal asked.

"*Confirmed. Heading down the funnel again, dumb bastards.*"

Volmar let go of his monitor and motioned for Two-ton to take the woman while he manned the wall. "Move her, quick."

"*It's a rainy day,*" the woman croaked.

"Sure it is," Two-ton moved past to grab her by the arm. "Just head this way . . ." As he tugged, her blanket opened up exposing a bulbous tumor-like belly with thick, scarred ridges and some taut, transparent flesh with liquids moving around beneath.

"*The fuck?*" Two-ton hissed.

The woman's head peeled open, but her flapping jaws continued to speak. Her jaws were filled with needlepoint teeth.

"*Rainy. Day.*"

Her gut exploded, throwing acid everywhere

Two-ton fell to the ground and rolled as he screamed, his armor melting onto his body.

Two-ton caught the brunt, but Volmar was still splashed. He got his arm up fast enough to catch most of the damage.

It felt like electricity surged through him as he stumbled back and hit the wall, his CAG melting away to expose red bubbling flesh.

"*Fuck, fuck!*" Volmar screamed. He rolled around and screamed.

But even through the panic, he noticed something worse.

The wall was hit.

The blast burned through the metal.

"*Hostiles inbound!*" someone roared over the call.

Volmar managed a weak hand to the call button. "*We're down, we're down!* The woman was hostile! She blew the barrier."

A voice came across the speaker, "*Shit, they're in here with us! They got inside the building!*"

Another frantic voice came on, "*Behind the—*" It cut off.

Volmar looked around the surrounding buildings where his team was. He saw blasts as shots fired. Across the street, there were flashes of gunfire, and then a soldier came flying out of a fifth-story window with a cronux on his back. He slammed into the ground and went still as the cronux ravaged him.

Volmar was too hurt to do anything, he only looked over the barrier as the creatures flooded into view. Waves larger than any he had yet to see.

This time it was different.

This time they had been smart.

THE JANISSARY WALKED through the open streets, the cronux surged past him, taking the breach. Before he'd arrived, they'd been a dumb and predictable horde, and the enemy had learned their ways.

But the Janissary knew theirs.

In the distant land of the Soviet Union, the enemy there had learned strategic warfare against the Janissary, and their fight had been a vicious one.

But this new enemy was unblooded, and the Janissary took advantage of that.

They hadn't expected his forces to silently move up into the buildings, or for one of his to get so close and breach the wall.

They broke the barrier now and flowed deeper into the city, while leapers took the roof, looking for aircraft.

This place was ripe for conquest.

And this war was easy.

11

Bao Kwan was in the unfortunate position of being too connected and not connected enough to do anything of importance within the Chinese military.

His uncle was a middling member of leadership within the Communist party, and while that conveyed some privileges, it also had some unfortunate side effects.

Kwan was able to enter the military at an advanced rank of his peers due to his uncle's position, despite his own lackluster scores. Kwan had all the right answers when it came to party doctrine, but any question about strategy, tactics, or technical expertise, and he faltered.

"You will be positioned as commander of a communications installation on the border with the Soviet Union. You will watch for the enemy, and you will be the eyes of the People's Republic."

Oh, his uncle certainly knew how to spit shine a turd. Kwan had, of course, become disappointed when his deployment listing was released, but his uncle certainly piqued his interest.

Eyes of the People's Republic.

What a load of shit.

In reality, the Chinese had built hastily constructed border defenses when it looked as if the Soviet Union would collapse, and the plague of demons would flow into China, but that was only a peripheral goal. The real focus had been on the outbreak in Beijing, and after that was contained, the government acted like it was no longer concerned with any invasion. They had the Dragon, so why be concerned? They were focused on expanding their interests in all directions.

Correction. In all directions except for the border with the Soviet Union.

Kwan had been left to rot as a commander of a small communications hub that had faulty wiring and a bad paint job.

They might as well have written *we don't give a shit* in big white letters on the side of the building.

The only thing respectable about it was a thick wall with guard towers made out of prefabricated metal lock walls. Kwan made sure to have a man on each guard post, not because it was necessary, but because if the wall was the only good thing he had, he sure as hell was going to make use of it.

Despite Kwan's boredom, things had gotten a tad more interesting in recent days. Before the situation in Beijing had gotten under control, the government had actually recalled border defenses, and while Kwan was only supposed to be manning a communications hub behind border defenses, he was instead ordered to do double duty as border units were drawn inward.

They would soon be replaced of course, but until then, Kwan had control of a scout patrol—a tank and a dozen or so men in CAG.

Sometimes Kwan liked to go outside and watch them hose down the tank. He would tell a few of the workers to make sure they got it clean.

Mentally, though, he would say to himself:

This is my first tank.

Later he was sure he would command many more in battle, or if not them, perhaps soldiers, or artillery, or something of importance.

But that's where those low test scores really came in to knuckle him, because when the tank patrol arrived, they awaited his orders.

There was an unfortunate problem. He wasn't sure what exactly a tank patrol was supposed to be doing on the border.

Patrolling of course, but he was sure there was more to it than that.

Everything had happened so quickly that no one had filled him in on his new duties or how to execute them.

He swallowed his pride and asked the tank captain.

"What did you do under your former commander?"

"We patrolled to make sure no enemy forces have crossed our borders. We looked for tracks or signs or in locations where aerial observation is impossible."

Then, with a voice that carried authority, Kwan had said, "You will continue to do so."

He wished it had been as easy as just that, but the details unraveled and apparently he had to assign a patrol route.

The tank captain explained that things were difficult as the patrol was understaffed, and the territory had deeply widened now with the withdrawal of forces, so they would have to do their best to pick the most obvious routes.

Kwan ordered the man to execute the designs and inform him of the plan, because his duties as the commander of the communications hub had not lessened simply because a tank patrol had arrived.

He let the captain take point in planning their routes, but he demanded that the man check in before and after leaving.

The patrols had been like clockwork, always back before dinner.

Except for today.

Kwan was outside smoking a cigarette. A cold chill in the air made him appreciate the high collar on his officer's jacket.

He looked out along the distant rock line.

The patrol was due back three hours ago, and now it was dark. The flood lights in the base made for poor visibility.

He pulled the cigarette from his mouth and exhaled through his nose. "Hail them again," he ordered one of his men.

"Yes sir," a man said before hurrying into the communications building.

Under better circumstances, there would be aerial patrols and satellite imaging of the border. But the aircraft had yet to be repositioned, and Kwan was not of suitable rank to call in for satellite imaging.

"Sir, there is still no response," the man said when he returned.

The lack of communications had not been worrying at first. The Soviet Union had equipment set up to block satellite imaging and foreign communications, and it was still active despite the collapse of the government. There were times when the patrol would head into a position where communications were difficult or impossible.

But it was never for hours at a time.

The end of his cigarette sizzled red in the night air as he considered what to do.

Should he send more men out to look? Or should he report to his superiors?

Or should he just give it another hour?

He flicked the cigarette out and snuffed it with his heel.

"Hail them again," he ordered for the third time this hour.

"Yes sir," the man hurried off.

Kwan stood there, fighting the urge to grind his teeth when the man called for him.

"Sir, we've connected with them! But there's a problem."

"What?" Kwan said, turning on his heels and storming forward.

He walked past the man and to the base door. He leaned forward for an eye scan and the scanner flashed green. The door receded into the wall and he entered.

An officer was already at the communications booth with a headset on speaking to the patrol. *"Say again? Cannot read you."*

Kwan stomped over and clicked the external speakers on the communications module.

A voice came alive that sounded both hoarse and deep.

"—contact . . . with enemy. Casualties sustained. Enemy forces—"

"Contact?" Kwan interrupted, and was surprised at the alarm within his voice. "Cronux?"

"Yes . . ." It was a single long, and hissing word.

"Estimated time of arrival?" Kwan barked.

"Approaching . . . Now."

The line dropped.

Kwan tapped a receiver button and heard an audible click but nothing else.

Casualties? Damage? What the hell was there to do now?

"You." Kwan pointed at the communications booth. "Go get a medical team and meet us outside." Kwan headed outside and hurried to a ladder on the wall. He climbed to the top and stepped onto the platform. A soldier with an open-air helmet sat in a chair and smoked a cigarette, staring out toward the hills and paying little attention to Kwan.

"You're early," he said with a casual glance back. When he saw that it was Kwan, he jumped up to his feet, his eyes went wide and he brought his hand up to a salute. He'd done it so fast that he forgot the lit cigarette in his mouth.

Kwan scowled and plucked the cigarette out of the man's mouth. "Man your post, we have a patrol incoming," he ordered and put the cigarette in his own mouth.

"Yes sir!"

Kwan puffed the cigarette and kept his eyes on the ridge.

He saw a speck in the distance.

"Give me your binoculars," Kwan said and held out his hand. The private handed them over and Kwan put them up to his eyes.

The binoculars came to life with the green shades of night vision. Kwan could see the tank rolling over the ridge. It was clear that it had damage, but it was hard to make out what precisely in the dark.

It looked like there were long jagged grooves down the side

The top cover was bent up too as it rolled in.

Three CAG armored soldiers were walking alongside it, their suits also damaged and muddied.

With his eyes still forward, he handed the binoculars over, and after the private took them, Kwan mindlessly pulled the cigarette out and handed that over too.

The private took it with some confusion before flicking it over the edge.

Kwan dug out his radio and pressed the call button. "Open the gate for the patrol team, they are arriving."

"Acknowledged," the voice on the other side said.

Kwan watched for a moment longer and held his hand out again to the private.

The private set his binoculars into Kwan's hand.

Kwan gave a confused look to it and thrust it back. *"Cigarette."*

The private jolted his chin up into the air. "Sir, I'm sorry, I tossed it over the side."

Kwan sneered and shoved the binoculars into the man's chest before heading to the ladder.

He climbed down, his leather-sole boots thumping against the cold metal.

Thunk-thunk-thunk.

The gate was already opening as he headed that way. "You! Go find maintenance and tell them to get the tank bed ready."

A private saluted and ran off.

Kwan went to stand in the middle of the gateway, his arms clasped behind his back as the tank slowly approached. He narrowed his eyes as the damage became more visible.

There had been a mess for sure. The CAGs were dented and scratched, but still usable. It looked like a plate or two had been completely removed, but it was hard to see with the mud.

The tank, on the other hand, with its hatch torn to hell, was no longer fit until they could get it repaired.

It was so irritating that Kwan felt the corner of his lip tug upward. There would be hell to pay for this. Even if the patrol was in a fight, there was no excuse at all for being unresponsive to calls.

Kwan practically had to fight the urge to storm toward them and reprimand them in the field.

But he steeled his patience and waited at the mouth of the base.

He intended to stop them before entering so he could more easily see the tank.

But just as he raised his leg to take a step forward, the tank growled like a wild beast and picked up speed, heading in faster than the CAG soldiers and leaving them behind.

He settled his leg back down but held his position at the mouth of the gate, but he felt an itch at his eye as it drew in, not slowing one bit.

He held up his hand and yelled, "Slow! *Slow!*"

The operators didn't hear them though, because if anything, they picked up speed.

"Slow dammit!" Kwan said with his hand still in the air.

The tank didn't slow.

Chunk-chunk-chunk.

The sound of the tank tread on the rocks grew louder as it closed in.

Kwan tugged his radio off his belt and pressed the call button.

But the tank was too fast, and Kwan lost his nerve before he could make the call, and half jumped out of the way as the tank rolled through the gate, leaving tracks in the soil where Kwan had just been standing.

The speeding tank came to an abrupt stop in the middle of the yard.

The bastards didn't even take it to the garage.

Kwan looked over and saw panicked men staring at him in disbelief.

Kwan tightened his face and yelled, "Turn off the vehicle!" But they hadn't heard him. He glanced out and saw the CAG soldiers closing, their rifles resting in their hands. He looked back to the tank again. "Shut it down!"

It ignored him still, and he felt the edges of his patience fray.

He couldn't be made to look stupid in front of the men. Regardless of the circumstances, he would be sure to have the tank operators beaten.

He shouted again and started walking toward the front of the tank. *"I said—"*

The tank fired and the ground shook.

75

Kwan found himself on the ground, his head spinning. He tried to lift his hand, but it shook.

With his mouth gaping open, he twisted his head and saw the fuel station in flames. The lights in the station had gone off and now only those fires illuminated the night.

Kwan couldn't hear anything more than an intense ringing.

He brought his shivering hand to his ear and it came back red.

His ears had blown.

He could feel the blood running down his neck now, like a bug with prickly legs crawling on his skin.

He tried to move his legs, but they didn't obey. All he could do was shift his head back and forth on the ground.

The CAG soldiers came in now, their rifles firing right overtop of Kwan.

Who were they shooting at? What was happening? Kwan was so confused, because none of it made any sense at all.

Then he saw insectile legs reach up from the hatch on the tank. A thin creature with a bulbous torso like some man-sized arachnid crawled out.

Kwan stared at it in disbelief before it leapt from the tank and out of his sight.

He tried to shift his head again, but his neck hurt too bad now, and he was sure he was dying. His head stayed in place, watching the hatch as he saw a hand reach out, and then an armored head come next.

CAG, but it wasn't Chinese.

Even dying, and in the dark of night with only a fire to assist, he knew the design. They'd showed it to him day after day while in training.

American.

The slender frame of a woman in CAG climbed out of the tank. She turned her attention toward Kwan. She climbed down from the tank, in no real hurry at all.

The flames and flashes of rifle fire threw shadows across her face as she walked up to Kwan.

She stopped at his feet, and there was nothing else Kwan could do but lay there and die.

She pressed the clasp on her helmet and it popped up with a burst of air.

She pulled it off, and Kwan recognized her.

The Red Bitch of Berlin.

He'd seen the videos of her in combat.

She was different now.

Purple veins climbed one side of her face, and she watched him with no concern or hate, as the wind caught her tangles of hair.

And her arm . . . it wasn't human.

Kwan's eyes blurred and he blinked, but even that was becoming hard. He tried to reach up to rub them, but now his hand refused to move.

He opened his mouth and he wanted to call for help, but all he did was hiss.

The Red Bitch leaned down toward him and put a finger on her lips.

"Shh."

She put her other hand, the inhuman one, around his neck and squeezed.

CHUNK-CHUNK-CHUNK.

The tank rolled around the yard of the compound as the fires grew. The hatch was torn off from when the cronux got in, and now the cool night air rolled inside as a dead man worked the controls with a hand that had several fingers bitten off. Another operator, his jaw missing, directed the movement.

Chunk-chunk-chunk.

The tank rolled behind Alice as the turret turned and looked for enemies.

She could feel them all: the operators and the infested CAG soldiers with their rifles held up right. The beasts inside them wanted to scream and frenzy, but she held the control. She gave them balance.

She could make them march.

The infested CAG soldiers tightened their grip on their rifles, as the parasites dug wisps deeper into the brain. They ran up platforms and aimed at the few remaining soldiers.

Alice saw through their eyes. She saw the fight unfolding.

But she turned her attention away.

Her focus was here, on the dead man in the officer's uniform before her.

She'd just crushed his throat, and now she was staring at her new hand.

It didn't feel real.

Unlike the other, this one bent in three places, and the fingers were long and clawed, and her skin rough with scales.

All at once, Alice started to breathe, her eyes widened as she stared at the arm and then at the man.

What had she done? What had she become?

Who was she?

A presence came over her, like a black cloud choking her soul.

She fell to her knees and stared up into the sky as a dark voice echoed inside her.

Love me.

The words were cold. They hurt.

It was hard to think.

It was easier to obey.

Alice looked back down to the dead officer and put her maligned hand around his throat again. She felt the wisps squirm out of her palm and cut into his neck. The dead man squirmed and danced, a puppet with the strings tightening.

And with a gasp, he came to life again.

Alice stood up, and the wisps sunk back into her hand. The dead man climbed to his feet with a drunken stagger.

With screams still in the air and rifles blasting, the dead man led Alice into the communications base.

He moved to the secure door and leaned forward, slapping a bloody hand down for support as he lined his eye up with the scan. The scanner came alive, running on backup power, and a green light went over his eyes as his mouth hung agape.

The signal on the door scan flashed green, and with a metal *clunk*, the door slid open.

Inside the base, red emergency lights flashed overhead as it ran on backup power.

The dead man shuffled inside and smacked into the wall and dragged his shoulder across it.

He had been the leader of this place once.

She could feel that in his mind. There were bits and pieces of who he had been, and she knew what he knew.

He threw his head back and moaned as a stem crawled out of his throat, gagging him. But he stayed on his feet and kept moving.

She followed behind him, her helmet in one hand, and an odd sense of deja vu washing over her.

The red emergency lights flashed and Alice blinked. She stopped walking.

She dropped her helmet and the *thud* it made against the metal floor made her jump.

Doubt and concern slid over her once more, but they came like a forgotten dream, one barely remembered in the waking hours.

Love me.

The voice came again, and when it spoke, Alice's soul rattled.

Love. She loved him, and he was a god, wasn't he?

What greater honor was there than to serve him?

To fight his war?

It was hard for Alice to think.

It was easy to obey.

She reached the long arm down and picked up her helmet. If those memories had been a dream, then she had woken from it, and now it faded into the abyss.

The dead man had continued down the hall, the red lights flashing on him, and a thin trail of blood behind him.

She followed once more and he led her to an emergency vid hub. It was a dead screen within a dark room. But the dead man knew how the backup power functioned for emergency communication. He shuffled over to the hub, his fingers working on the keys even as his head rolled around his neck and made gagging noises while the stem slithered out further.

The console came to life, and words in Chinese strung across it.

Alice didn't know the language, but the dead man did. He shifted his position, and with his head still craned up, one eye rolled around until it could see the screen.

He pressed a few commands and a red light lit up on the screen.

The recording functions had begun.

Alice stood in front of it and the dead man came to her side.

She understood the enemy.

This would be a new kind of war.

12

ZHAO SAT ALONE in his office. The lights were dimmed and his hands were folded on the desk as he talked on a communications screen with Dr. Feng, China's top brain and cybernetic surgeon.

Dr. Feng bowed his head and looked up, a single cybernetic eye adjusting and refocusing to the light on his screen. *"The Dragon has undergone many changes, Chairman, and not all of them are our doing."*

"I've been informed, but I would like to hear them again from your perspective, doctor."

The doctor gave a thin smile. Clearly he was nervous. Zhao had that effect on people.

"The Dragon's medical team informed me that he was undergoing massive changes. In fact, he ejected his lungs through his mouth some time ago."

Zhao had, of course, already heard this. He'd even seen the discarded lungs himself. But there were still many questions. "And how is it that he was able to continue breathing and speaking?"

The doctor's eye twisted and focused, a single red dot in the center of it. *"I'm sorry, Chairman, but such things are not my field of study, I am a cybernetics—"*

Zhao interrupted. "You have a better understanding of such things than most, and I've already heard the opinions of others. What have you concluded?"

"Simply put, Chairman, we do not know."

Zhao cleared his throat in response and gestured for the doctor to continue.

"His changes, though rapid at the time, are even more so now. His muscle tissue is altering, and new organs are growing that we haven't identified. The growth itself is a pace unseen in nature. And we don't know why this is happening."

"I know why," Zhao said without adjusting his posture. "It was because he killed an Archon and ate its brain. I'm told that he dug it out of the creature's skull with his fingers and they found bits of it beneath his nails. We don't know what that did to him, but certainly, it did *something*."

Dr. Feng, still grinning wildly, bobbed his head in agreement.

Zhao enjoyed respect, but fear could be an annoyance.

"You have yet to identify the new organs, but have you done any studies on them?"

"Subvisual scans and preliminary probing. There are no clear analogous organs within human bodies, though I've conferred with the team that studied the Archon's corpse, and it too has these strange organs. Other species of the cronux, however, do not. At least those that we have studied. It appears to be something for a certain class of cronux."

"The Dragon is not a cronux. He is their master, but he is human, and he is Chinese."

"Of course." The doctor turned his eyes away for a moment. *"The organs appear vestigial, but that seems highly unlikely for a nonfunctioning organ to grow both within the Archon and within the Dragon, though such vestigial organs can be found in nature, so it is plausible. We tried to collect cells from the organs, but there were signs that it affected the Dragon's health monitoring, and thus too dangerous to attempt."*

"That was wise. The Dragon is too precious to be risked in any way." Zhao gestured once more. "Show me what you've done."

"Of course." Dr. Feng hit a few commands and his face was gone and a new screen showed a digital layout of the Dragon's body. Feng

guided a marker across the screen as he explained. *"If you look here, Chairman, you will see that we have established a cranial sub platform to house the Dragon's brain, and we covered it with an armored dome."* The screen showed a large round helmet with two bulbous sides that covered all of Erkin's head but his mouth. To Zhao, it looked similar to the head of a praying mantis.

Feng pressed some commands and the screen adjusted to show brain scans. *"Additional visual sensors were wired into his brain. The cranial dome will now provide three hundred and sixty degree vision to the Dragon, while also providing protection. A lower mouth plate can be added if you wish, but we've thought it best to take the adjustments in stages where possible."*

"Yes," Zhao agreed. "But what of the concerns of psychosis? Will the new sensory input overload his mind?"

"That will not be a problem." The video feed slid up to the two large balloonish areas on either side of the helmet. *"Since the gunshot wound destroyed much of his skull and caused massive swelling, we opted to separate large chunks of it altogether, and store the soft tissues here in the sub platforms. In addition, North Japanese research helped us place secondary life support systems in the dome that would keep his brain oxygenated for a short time even if there was heart failure. Essentially, we should be able to bring him back to life, or in a worst case scenario, relocate the brain into a new construct, though that's unclear how effective he would remain or if his abilities would endure."*

"The support systems connected to his brain will not impair his cognitive abilities?"

"The impact will be minimal, but there may be some changes."

"To be more clear, doctor, will he be able to wipe his own ass?"

Taken by surprise, the doctor had a nervous chuckle. *"Heh, certainly, certainly. He will remain fully functional and independent. The North Japanese have been conducting a lot of research on bisecting the brain and the extent to where the sections can be moved and still kept functional."*

The doctor tapped a portion of the screen with a small line protruding from the brain. *"This synthetic nerve stem will also make the additional arm functional. In time, he should be able to move it as fluidly as his original arms, but there will be an adjustment period. Although some past experiments ended with the nervous system shutting down and cognitive failure in the subjects when performing the surgery on areas of the brain that were alpha critical, we were sure to avoid these sections and conduct ourselves on the dispensable portions. Should any issues arrive, the subcerebral implants have a relief function that will manage stress levels."* The screen returned to Dr. Feng's face. *"In short, he may not provide much of an enjoyable conversation, but he will be quite effective on the battlefield. And he should . . . be able to clean himself."*

"Excellent. When will he awaken?" Zhao asked.

"We expect three to four more days of fluid transfers and nerve rehabilitation before waking the Dragon."

"The delay is inconvenient but acceptable."

Zhao's office door opened, and his secretary entered.

"Chairman," she spoke, her voice a quiver as she tipped her head and waited to be addressed.

Feng frowned in confusion on the screen, but Zhao turned from him.

"What is it?" Zhao asked.

"We have received a video," the secretary answered.

"Of *what?*" Zhao said with more insistence.

She glanced up and flashed a look toward Feng, then back to Zhao.

"Alice Winters. She sent a message to our people."

Zhao's jaw tightened, but he turned his attention back to the screen. "Doctor Feng, report any change in status to me." He reached over and hit the button to end the call without waiting for a response. "Send me the video."

The secretary deepened her bow and backed out of the room.

Zhao clasped his hands in front of him once more.

The screen came alive again.

A demon stared back at him.

Zhao leaned forward in the chair with his elbows on his knees.

Alice Winters, her skin as pale as a corpse, spoke in a chilled and emotionless voice.

"Those that submit will live. Those that do not will die. We will burn your cities to the ground. We will take your bodies. You now belong to us."

"Freeze," Zhao commanded and the video stopped.

Alice Winters stared at him. Her eyes were soulless.

Except for the helmet and a missing arm piece, she was suited in CAG, but he could see the purple veins ran up one side of her neck and snaked around her left eye. One arm was barely visible, but it was clearly something inhuman—dark rigid flesh that was hard to make out in the vid.

Why was she so different from any of the others? Why was she smarter and able to communicate?

He didn't know. Nor did he know why she would be willing to take any alive.

But even so, he watched the video again.

"Repeat," he ordered the vid.

Alice Winters' hollow voice came alive again, *"Those that submit will live. Those that do not will die. We will burn your cities to the ground. We will take your bodies. You now belong to us."*

The Red Bitch of Berlin wasn't dead, she was alive and coming for him.

And The Dragon was still down.

"Trace call signal," he commanded the computer and a series of coordinates came up. "Transfer location to General Chen in missile command. Issue with command words: *Jade, Spear, Long Wind.*"

The screen flashed with a bar as the commands were being sent.

Zhao intended to burn that place to the ground, but somehow, he knew it wouldn't be enough.

He reached over and hit the call button for his secretary.

"*Sir?*" she responded.

"Open the call with Dr. Feng once more."

"Dragon? Can you hear me?"

It was a voice somewhere distant.

"Can you hear me, Dragon?" Someone snapped their fingers a few times.

Erkin slowly opened his eyes, but it was hard to see anything. The light felt too bright.

"Dragon? You will be disoriented. We had to wake you early."

"*Ehh?*" Erkin wheezed, too weak to speak.

"His vitals are in, he's stable," another voice said.

"Excellent," the man said.

Erkin blinked again and the fog began to lift.

There was a doctor in a cap and gown with a cybernetic eye in the chair before him.

"There was an accident. You were shot and nearly died, but we were able to perform surgery. We saved you," the doctor explained. He blinked with one eye but not the other. The cybernetic eye only tightened, its red center staying constantly focused.

"*Wha—*" Erkin took a deep breath and licked his lips. "*Water.*"

"In time. But we need to explain a few things."

Erkin's head was heavy, he felt it slump to his shoulder. He slowly twisted to look around the room, but his whole body felt odd.

The doctor motioned with a hand. "Please, just focus on me, I need to explain. *There have been some changes.*" Wrinkles formed around the man's eyes as he grinned.

Erkin's mouth gaped open as needle-prick pain jolted through his spine. It started at the base and climbed up to his skull, like a sharp point going in and out to touch each nerve. It caught him so quickly he couldn't do anything but freeze in place.

The doctor furrowed his brow. "You're in pain? That shouldn't be possible, you're on a sedative."

Erkin moaned and reached to his mouth.

His fingers rubbed something metal and cold around his head. He reached with both hands to feel around the edges.

Something heavy was strapped around his head.

"*He's moving,*" the doctor shouted. "You were supposed to sedate him!"

"I did," another person said in disbelief.

The doctor came out of his seat and pointed at someone. "Turn on the nerve functions, he needs his medications."

There was a loud whine, and an electrical shock went through Erkin that made every muscle tighten.

He threw his head back and howled.

The world began to spin, and so did Erkin's head. It felt so heavy and unbalanced, he grabbed the metal with his hands and tried to hold it in place.

"*Ease yourself.* You are okay! Sit back," the doctor commanded. "You're going to have trouble adjusting."

Erkin couldn't blink. He couldn't close his eyes.

"We've added a third eye," the doctor said with something close to glee.

Erkin dug his fingers at the helmet, but all he did was scratch his nails across the metal.

"See?" the doctor pointed.

Erkin looked up and saw himself on a monitor screen. A large metal dome was fitted around his head down to his nose, bulbous on both sides like the head of some insect. There was a small surgical bed next to him with a thin multi-jointed limb resting on it.

Erkin turned away from the screen and looked to his side. He saw both what was behind and in front of him. The disorientation almost made him topple out of the chair.

Instead, he focused on the surgical bed.

The multi-joined arm rested there. It shifted and moved as Erkin did.

"We've also attached a tooled appendage. This will greatly improve your effectiveness."

Erkin twisted his head back and forth, and the optical lenses tightened and refocused with the movement. He could see the doctor, the back of the chair, the walls, the machines hooked up to him, and the glaring eyes of the staff.

All waiting.

All watching.

The doctor held up a hand to steady Erkin. "I know, it will take some time to be fully functional, but believe me, it is an improvement. You will have three hundred and sixty degree vision, along with an arm that functions as well as your other two—better even. The three fingers are flex-jointed and can open or close to either side of the hand. We did have to remove your eyes, so you will have to adapt to the new field of vision, and the fact that you will no longer blink. There will be some optical strain at first, but you will adjust, and of course, there were some unforeseen problems. We did wire in pain control measures, but by evidence of your pain and resistance to sedatives, your unique biology makes it difficult to anticipate any—"

"*Why?* Why would you do this to me?" Erkin's voice quivered, and if he could still cry he would have.

The doctor twisted his head, confused. "We've saved you —*improved* you. I'm sure this is all stunning. We would have let your body take time to adjust to the implants, but we have run out of time and had to wake you up."

Erkin licked his lips. "My wife, where is my wife?"

The doctor shook his head. "I know nothing about her. I do not handle those affairs." One of his eyes blinked—the mechanical eye did not.

Erkin moved to stand and felt the sharp pain in his side. He twisted toward it, but that only made it worse, like hands inside his guts, squeezing into a fist.

"Wait, wait! We need to disconnect you from the instruments. We did not anticipate you on your feet so quickly." He glanced toward some staff members and they rushed toward Erkin's back. It was dizzying. He could both see the doctor and the staff behind him, unlocking him from the machines. "Let us assist. You must be careful, you are too valuable until we have more Dragons."

The pain rolled away as Erkin twisted his head. "More?"

"This too is not my purview, but operations are underway as we speak. You will have allies soon."

A staff member unhooked Erkin's third arm. Without moving his head, he could see it to the side of him. It flexed up, rising from the table like a snake. The three thin fingers opened and closed as if to stretch.

They were plastic and metal, and it didn't matter that there were metal wires for veins because he could feel it like an arm that was going numb.

Erkin stood up fully, and the staff scrambled behind him to disconnect the tubing as some snapped out of his back. Someone knocked over a tray and the instruments clattered to the ground.

The doctor, still in his chair, tensed as Erkin loomed over him.

"Why did you do this to me?" Erkin asked.

"This is not my—"

"*Why?*" The mechanical arm rose up along his side with a quiet whine.

The doctor shrank into his seat and held his arms up.

"Chairman Zhao ordered it. There is a new threat arriving. I don't know what it is. But your assistance is needed for the People's Republic."

Erkin twisted his head to look around the room, but that was only by instinct. Doing so made him further disoriented as his eyes saw everything.

He focused on the screen and saw the robotic nightmare he'd become reflected back.

He could imagine the gleeful smiles of the doctor as they opened him up. While he lay on the bed, his spine and brain exposed, they probed and cut where they wanted—just children with a new toy to take apart. Were his eyes in some plastic bag somewhere deep within the trash?

What hadn't they taken from him?

First his family.

Then his mind.

Now his body.

He wouldn't give them his soul.

A darkness curled inside his stomach. All the technicians in the room watched with fearful eyes, and it made his skin prickle.

They thought he was a monster, and they were afraid.

They would know. They made him that way.

He felt movement deep within his gut, he imagined a cluster of swollen slugs slithering inside him.

They were wrong. He wasn't a monster.

He was something more.

He glared down at the doctor, his body already steadying to the adjustments. He could feel the things in his gut slithering up his chest.

"What do you think I am?" he asked in a voice that betrayed calmness.

Confused, the doctor glanced at the others and shrank back in his seat.

"You are the savior of China. You are the Dragon."

He stomped a bare foot forward and screamed, "I don't want to be a Dragon! I'm a *father*. I'm a *husband*. *I want my family*. Who will give them to me?"

The doctor shook his head. "I don't know anything about them."

Erkin held up a finger to silence him. "*Where are the others?*"

The doctor shook his head. "The others?"

"The other *Dragons*? Where are they?"

"I don't—" the doctor started but Erkin's mechanical arm snapped out and grabbed him, the flex fingers squeezing around his throat.

The doctor pawed at the metal limb and kicked. The chair slid out from behind him and Erkin had to step forward to hold the struggling man's weight.

The staff panicked and screamed. Erkin saw every one of them, his new eyes allowing him to see the entire room at once. They scrambled backward, knocking things over as they moved toward the door.

"Where are they?" Erkin demanded again, his lips curling to show his teeth.

The doctor choked out words. "*Don't. Know.*"

One of Erkin's flex fingers extended and wrapped up the back of the doctor's neck. It tightened.

There was a loud pop as his neck cracked and the sound of metal on the floor as the pressure made the doctor's synthetic eye pop out. It bounced and rolled under a desk. Blood oozed through the tears on the doctor's neck.

A woman rushed past, but Erkin snatched her by the wrist and pulled her close.

He pulled her head aside, and with instinct alone, sunk his teeth into her neck.

He felt one of those swollen slugs within his gut slither right up his throat and into the woman's neck.

Erkin dropped her and others screamed and ran past while the woman rolled around on the floor, her mind dissolving into madness.

Barefoot, Erkin walked toward the exit, his metal arm still dragging the doctor along the floor, leaving a long, red streak. Erkin dropped the dead man in the doorway. He could see down both sides of the corridor without so much as moving his head.

A group of soldiers rounded the corner with open-face helmets and chest plates. They had their clubs drawn, but their pistols were still holstered. They shouted commands to stop, but Erkin paid them no mind.

He was too busy reaching out, his mind spreading across the hive mind to find the parasites.

The ones being used in the Dragonskin program.

"*There,*" he said out loud.

PROFESSOR GHAO WAS at the height of biological engineering and research. Just recently, she was overseeing a project aimed toward splicing animal cells of various species together to make more useful meat animals. The research was showing progress, and the importance of a stable food supply to China was so great that she was ordered to continue even when the alien invasion began.

That's why it was such a surprise when the government swooped in one day and told her she was being reassigned to a new military project.

When they came for her, she was not given even an hour to pack her bags, or to bid farewell to her husband. She was immediately gathered and transported by helicopter to the capital. Agents stuffed a datapad into her hands and she spent the entire flight reading about the newly designed project.

Dragonskin was now the top priority of the Chinese government.

They had started with the most loyal and capable of the Chinese military, but the complete failure to produce even a single success proved to be an utter waste of resources.

When she reported her failure, she expected that she would be removed from the project altogether.

Instead, she was ordered to increase the volume of participants.

It had been months now since she'd even spoken to her husband, but that didn't matter.

The project slowed for no one. It continued even while she slept. There was endless screaming, day and night.

All for China.

Ghao worked tirelessly until she produced a success: Erkin Kahn, the *Dragon*.

He had proved mighty in the war against the intruders, beyond what the party leaders had even hoped. He stopped the assault on Beijing, turned the enemy back, and then confronted the enemies of China.

He was a dragon in whole.

Like a proud mother, Ghao watched the vidfeeds of him in battle, walking with a divine level of calm, his hands held out to his sides with the palms aimed to the heavens while the demons of Hell flowed around him.

She knew that this had all been worth it. All the pain and blood bore fruit.

And it would again.

The project doubled, and as the internment camps emptied, new volunteers were needed. They scoured orphanages, opiate dens, bars, hospitals, and some were simply collected directly from the street.

All for the defense of China. The People's Republic would never fall, and Ghao would play some small part in that.

Now she stood at a one-way window on the second floor of the ad hoc medical lab and oversaw the experiments—a bloody, tireless business set up in an empty gymnasium. Walls of plastic sheets were set up to divide rooms. It kept the blood from spraying too far, but it did nothing for the screams.

It didn't matter. Just last night she'd been standing at this same window, watching a woman thrash about in her bed as the parasite took her. Ghao had seen it countless times, but somehow, in some way, she knew this one was different.

She watched closely, ignoring all other things.

After a moment, the woman had gone still. The technician at the bed waited a full minute before grabbing the woman's bed and preparing to wheel her body to the incinerator.

But Ghao pressed the call button on her receiver.

"Tell bed thirty-four to delay disposal."

A voice had responded. *"Confirmed."*

It was only thirty seconds later that the woman began to move.

Another Dragon had been born.

The woman was immediately transferred out of the lab and the work continued.

Had they finally broken the code? Had Ghao distilled the project down to a repeatable procedure?

For the moment, all she could do was stand at the window and wait for the birth of another Dragon.

She saw a man go still, and there was a stirring inside her, just like the day before. Somehow she could see it in a way her mind had yet to understand.

The man's eyes were open and staring up with a dead man's glare.

But that couldn't happen. The parasites didn't kill that way. They either took over, or they were conquered.

Something must have changed.

But she noticed the syringe in the technician's hand.

He hadn't injected the parasite.

The man, for whatever reason, had gone completely still without the injection.

What did it mean? Had the man defeated the parasite on his own? She theorized such things were possible, but she'd never seen it.

But could it be? Two born in less than twenty-four hours?

Or maybe, he simply died and that's all there was.

The technician waited a minute, and then a minute more, the syringe still in his hand. Perhaps he too felt something?

Whatever it was, it must have passed. He approached the man, readying to inject the parasite.

Ghao pressed the button on the receiver.

"Instruct bed twenty-seven not to conduct injection. Instead he is to bring the volunteer in for closer observation."

"Confirmed," the operator replied.

She watched the technician put a hand to his ear and listen to the new commands. He set his syringe aside and walked over to the bed. He unlocked the buckles that connected it to the base wall and pulled the bed loose. He pushed it out into the main hall.

The man on the bed looked peaceful, as if there hadn't been some intense struggle for his soul just now.

Ghao stared without daring to blink, her instincts telling her something had changed.

She put her hand to the glass and leaned closer.

ERKIN WALKED DOWN THE HALLWAY, the hospital floor tile cold beneath his feet. His body was here, but his mind was in another place entirely.

He found the parasites, not far from him, and he felt one go into a man.

He held it still.

"Stop!" a black-armored guard ordered Erkin, a nightstick in his hand.

More guards came, and Erkin could see them all, both in front and behind.

One charged, his weapon raised, and Erkin's third arm struck out, the fingers narrowed into an edge.

It caught the man in the throat and he stumbled back, hands to his neck, as his weapon clattered to the floor.

Others rushed in, but didn't they know Erkin had changed? He had slain the Jade Archon, eaten its brain, and thrown up his own lungs.

He wasn't a man anymore.

So what were their weapons to Erkin?

What were such things to a *god*?

The infected woman sprang out of the operating room, her face already a spider's web of purple veins. The open wound on her neck had a lashing tentacle.

Erkin paid her little mind as he snatched one man and threw him into a wall. The third arm shot out and hit the man in the shoulder, pinning him still. Erkin planted a leg alongside the wall with one hand at the man's wrist and the other at the elbow.

He pulled hard enough that the arm tore free from the shoulder.

Screams filled the hallway, and Erkin beat the next man to death with a bloody arm.

Another ran in, apparently the bravest of what remained, and Erkin kicked him in the chest hard enough that he heard it crack.

The infected woman was beaten to the ground by two armored men, their clubs raining crushing blows down onto her head.

Erkin could see it all, and more still in places far beyond.

For in this world, he had many eyes.

Erkin's metal arm reached over and grabbed the soldier from the back. He dragged the man close, and the uneven weight made Erkin stagger a few feet.

The man struggled but Erkin clenched his chin and wrenched his head back to expose his neck. With only his thumb, Erkin dragged his nail across the man's skin, making him howl as blood dripped out.

Erkin only opened his mouth and the parasite came lashing out, its wisps a fury as it grabbed onto the man and went into the wound.

Erkin dropped him to the floor with a clatter. The man rolled around and bucked as he fought the inevitable.

More soldiers came, shouting and pointing. Erkin killed them and barely noticed their presence.

He was there in body, but not in mind.

He was with the man in the bed, a parasite crawling through his veins, but one that held still.

One that slept and waited for the prey.

The man's eyes were open with a dead man's stare, and Erkin saw a technician in a hazmat suit some feet away. The technician held a hand to his ears as if answering a call. He held a syringe in one hand, just like the kind they had pumped into Erkin.

The technician sat the syringe down and approached, and while he did, the parasite's wisps stretched and crawled through the man's body, finding his way into the nutrient-rich brain and heart and sucking away the proteins.

But Erkin held it still. The body didn't move or animate.

The technician reached past the bed to unhook locks connecting it to a base wall to keep it stabilized. He yanked the bed free and wheeled it out of the enclosure.

Erkin pulled back his hold and let the parasite wake up.

Proteins and nutrients surged together into one of the parasite's wisps and it shot out of the infected man's mouth with such sudden growth that men would have thought it impossible.

It speared into the technician, cutting right through the plastic hazmat suit and into his chest. The technician collapsed to his knees and screamed as he became infected.

Erkin pulled his focus from the parasite as he felt it spread, and he reached to all the others there in the lab.

One was small and crawling out of a canister. Erkin grabbed hold of it and made it turn back on the technician. It latched onto the man's face as he slapped at it, but a flame soldier scorched them both.

Another connected into a woman who wasn't properly belted down, and Erkin helped her get a hand free—that was all she needed.

A handful of parasites jumped from their canisters and scurried across the ground, their wisps. Someone stomped on one, but another found its way into a corpse waiting to be put in the incinerator.

There were more still and now they didn't move with animal instinct, but under Erkin's careful guidance.

Most burned, and some died, but a few were loose, and that was all that was needed.

An infected woman had her head arched down and ran barefoot through the gymnasium, a tentacle lashing out from her back.

A man pinned to his bed had a technician by the arm, pulling him and biting through the flimsy suit.

One thrashed about, knocking over plastic walls, as it burned from the fires of a flame trooper.

Erkin felt it all—his presence filled the room.

But here, with his body, Erkin had made his way down to the ground floor and now stepped from the hospital, towing a dead man in one hand. The once men followed behind him, some screaming and others following in silent devotion.

Erkin put his foot on the pavement and looked up at the high-rise buildings in Beijing, but he settled his gaze toward the laboratory not far away.

If they wouldn't give him his wife and daughter back, then he would take everything from them.

13

MOLLER LOOKED out the helicopter window as it hovered over the old, massive post office in New York. After the invasion in the city, the military took command of it and several other federal buildings to set up a base of operations.

But it was hardly ideal.

The military had seized choke points leading into the city, and erected large concrete barriers and fencing, and now lines of refugees were awaiting entry.

Not far from the refugees, a steel-plated gate leading into New York slid aside and three armored troop carriers rolled into the city followed by four tanks. Countless others were milling about the barrier, all preparing to enter the city or strengthen the defense.

Moller had on a headset so she could hear the pilots over the roar of the helicopter. The headset had a visor attachment that she flipped down. She rubbed her finger over the dial to make the lenses zoom.

Lines of beaten, bloodied, and starving people were crowding around just outside the gates. Soldiers lined them up and pointed toward inspection officers that gave each person a look over before letting them in.

There was no close inspection.

"How's it look?" the copilot's voice buzzed in through the headset over the roar of the engine. *"Think we're fittin' to kick some ass?"*

Moller panned over the people. One man stood by himself, his face an emotionless stone. Any one of them could be a chimera.

Moller pressed the communications button on the headset. "I don't think anyone down there knows what the hell they're getting into. I wouldn't look to stick around if I were you."

"Not a problem," the pilot's voice came on now. *"Base cleared us for fifteen minutes. This is a dump and go."*

"Not going to refuel?" she asked.

"Can't. The landing zone is too small, and they need the space. They told us to get back to Lancaster and refuel. They have a liaison down there to meet you though. Hang tight now, we're putting it down." The copilot turned back and gave her a grin.

"Got it," she said and leaned back in her seat.

The helicopter descended to the ground, and Moller got out. She headed off the landing zone before turning to watch a crew rush over to unload her gear: two metal cases.

Everything else she needed was in a bag slung over her shoulder, but the metal cases had her new CAG: an experimental weapon system devised from the data they'd collected in Moscow.

Roles had told her all about it back in Washington. *"The data tells us that the radiation at the Moscow bunker dulled their senses. We used the same alloys in the armor. We think this will make you harder to see."*

"Are you sure it'll work?" she'd asked.

He hadn't even paused.

"No. This'll be the first live test. Report your findings."

She was being sent to a war zone with untested armor and a handful of experimental weapons.

"Lovely," she mumbled as she watched the landing team, fitted with armored lift supports, pick up the cases and move them away.

"Agent Moller!" a man called to her as he walked in her direction. He was wearing military fatigues. "I'm Major Evans, your liaison. We just got reports that you landed. The colonel has a meeting planned with you tonight, but I'm supposed to show you the perimeter of the base. If you follow me, I will—"

"I don't want to see the perimeter." Moller shook her head as she looked over the base. She turned to look the major in the eyes. "I want to see where you're keeping the civilians."

MOLLER STEPPED up onto the roof of the old post office. The sky had turned gray and looked like it may rain at any moment. Moller glanced up at it with some irritation that she didn't bring a hat.

Major Evans stepped one leg up to the ledge and gestured down. "There it is, Moller. Our largest processing tent."

At that angle, Moller could see just to the edge of the inside of the large tent. Long tables were set up and people waited in line to enter and then they exited to another line where a convoy of trucks waited to be filled and left one at a time.

Moller felt the pit of her stomach tighten. "What are you doing there?"

The major narrowed his gaze down to the tent. "Hand out disaster supplies, mostly blankets and some rations. Then we take down their names, contact information, and next of kin to provide to our disaster relief partners."

"How many have been through here?"

The major shook his head. "Our zone specifically? Hard to say, but we work day and night. With this tent and all the others along the access points, I believe it's close to a million plus. Maybe just over."

She pointed. "Where are those trucks going?"

"To shelters, but I can't tell you precisely which ones. This whole goddamn plan has been weaved together as fast as we could."

"Those shelters—are they under military guard?"

The major glanced away to consider, and nodded his head. "Believe so, but I haven't been out there. It's only for those that don't have anywhere else to go."

A chill rolled across Moller's skin. "What do you mean?"

"Some of them go stay with family or head off to find a hotel."

"*No.*" Moller shook her head. "How many have been released?"

The major stiffened his back too and stepped off the ledge. "*Released* isn't the right word, Agent Moller. We're not the goddamn Russians. Those people are American citizens and we aren't allowed to detain them beyond a reasonable transfer from the disaster area."

Moller showed her teeth and looked back across the crowds.

So many faceless people. An endless crowd that might as well be one blob.

Any one of them could be one of the chimera.

"Where's the colonel? I need to see him *right now.*"

"He's in the middle of fighting a war. He's going to—"

"Get me in the room with him right now, or I call President Winters and tell him none of you have time for a meeting."

THE COLONEL HAD his arms crossed as he listened to Moller, a digital map screen of a nearby section of New York glowed beneath him, casting blue light up to his face. He'd been irritated with the interruption but agreed to meet her.

Moller stood at the other side of the table; she folded her hands behind her, but kept eye contact with the colonel. "The chimera are a breed of cronux that can look human. Our initial understanding of them is that they do not communicate effectively, and lack genitalia, but they can spread the parasites as effectively as others of their race. The White House and the intelligence community believe this is how they were able to penetrate so deeply into Europe. Effectively, they create refugee situations and then send the chimera in with the fleeing populace, and the confusion gives them cover. It's precisely what's happening here. Everyone needs to be detained, and thoroughly checked. Any one of them could be chimera."

The colonel uncrossed his arms and pointed at the screen. "Agent Moller, do you recognize this map?"

She looked down at the screen and saw roads and buildings, but nothing she recognized. "No sir, I do not."

"This is the northern portion of Staten Island." He gestured to a connector point. "This is the Eisenhower passway. This is where we are." He waved a hand over the map. "This is where the half a million civilians are that we're currently trying to evacuate." He tapped the connector again. "Over *one* bridge. We've closed in on two hundred thousand, but any delay means those buildings here, here, and here are going to stay populated. Those people will be inside when the fighting starts." He waved his arms out to his side. "Beyond that, we don't have housing for the ten million people of New York. We don't have enough food, transportation, or living space." He waved a hand between the two of them. "When I was overseas, we'd get suits from Washington that'd want to come over and tell us how to do our job. They always want to talk about land, bullets, and bodies, they never want to talk toilets to shit in, because that's where wars are really won and lost—logistics. If you don't have a place for people to shit then you don't have a place to keep them. I believe every word you're saying, and understand it, but I don't know what it is you want me to do about it. If you're here representing the White House, then you need to tell them this situation is untenable and we'll need further instruction and resources."

Moller let out a breath and leaned off the table. "I understand."

The colonel nodded his head. "I'll instruct the processing to do the best they can, but what you're asking me to do is order a bunch of civilians down there to undress in crowded tents and let the military look them over." He rubbed his tongue across his teeth and shook his head. "No one is going to understand why, and it's going to slow things down, but I'll do what I can. Even then, every extra step will slow things down, and the enemy has broken through our line on numerous occasions. We slow things down too much and we're going to end up leaving hundreds of thousands of people over as those things pour in."

"They've breached your exterior line?"

"Not into Staten Island, but the reports are that Queens is Hell on

Earth, and Brooklyn is going to fall next. The general's forces have blown most of the bridgeways into Manhattan, but they're still dealing with mass evacuations." He gestured over the screen and the map zoomed out. He tapped on a portion further north. "Here the military became engaged while conducting evacuations. There was a drawback of forces and now civilians are stuck behind the line."

Moller clenched her teeth and shook her head. "We were getting reports that they were being held back?"

"Tactics changed. They went from dumb beasts to tactical maneuvers and caught us by surprise in a few key areas, and there's something big up there."

Moller nodded and looked down at the screen. "The tactics just began changing recently?"

The colonel snapped his fingers. "Like that." He gestured toward the screen again. "General McClain is getting the bridge to Brooklyn rigged up, and we're going to blow it after we've finished evacuations." He clenched his teeth and shook his head. "We're surrendering the Statue of Liberty."

"How have the breaches affected the planned naval landings?"

The colonel shook his head. "Our forces are preparing now. We evacuate the populace, pull back and let them spread their numbers, then conduct our landing to squash what remains."

"I need to be there when it happens."

"When what happens?"

"The landing." Moller planted her hands down on the map again.

The colonel scoffed. "We're conducting evacuations, we can't allow non-military in. You don't even have a CAG."

She looked up at him. "I know what I'm doing and I have presidential clearance for all my actions. I went in and out of the Soviet Union, and I've fought them before. I have a better handle on what we're dealing with than anyone else on this side of the planet. I need to go in there and see what happened, and what's going on back in their nest." She waved her hand around Long Island. "And I brought my own CAG." She looked up at him, the map light on her face.

"But I'm going to need a ride."

14

MILES TOOK A DEEP BREATH, puffing up his cheeks and slowly blowing out the air.

He had jitters just like the first time he went on TV.

No, it wasn't that bad was it? He'd almost pissed down his leg that time. He'd learned a valuable lesson that day—always be sure to take a piss before the cameras start rolling.

Well the cameras weren't rolling now, but he was about to meet the president of the United States.

Fortunately, he'd remembered to empty his bladder before sitting down in the waiting room.

The blonde had left to provide crucial advice in New York—apparently things were going to Hell there and they needed an expert, so they sent her. Miles believed it, she seemed competent enough, and twice as easy to look at. But he wished she was here.

She seemed like she knew what she was doing, and he could think of shit all for good reasons as to why he was here.

"How do my teeth look?" Kevin asked, grinning wide enough to show every tooth.

"Like a million bucks, mate." Miles slapped him on the back, and plastered on a smile.

Kevin, the poor bastard, seemed like he was about to have a nervous breakdown.

Miles was too, but at least he was good at hiding it.

"You think he'll like us?" Kevin asked.

"What's not to like?" Miles said. "You're a—"

"The shit—" Marat said, sitting across from them, one leg bouncing. "I have no cigarette."

Miles frowned. "Bad form to smoke in the White House anyway, comrade. We'll get you a smoke after we are out."

Marat glanced at the ground and chewed his lip.

Kevin breathed hard, big deep breaths.

"The hell you so stressed out for, mate? The worst he can do is call us a couple useless bastards and send us home. Not like he's going to eat you."

"You're not nervous?" Kevin asked.

"Course, but no use telling everyone about it."

Kevin shook his head.

"Tell you what, how about a joke?" Miles glanced between the two of them.

"Joke?" Marat narrowed his eyes as if he were unsure.

"Yeah, get a little laugh to loose'n the gears before we go in."

"Okay, okay. Let's hear it." Kevin bobbed his head.

"All right." Miles grinned and leaned in—he pointed at Marat. "Focus in here, comrade, you'll love this. What do you call a communist with two dollars in his pocket?" He looked between the two and they focused. "I don't know, I never met one."

Marat furrowed his brow. "I don't understand."

Kevin widened his eyes and shook his head. "That's dark, man."

"What?" Miles laughed under his breath. "That joke isn't dark."

"What does it mean?" Marat asked.

Kevin huffed. "He's making a joke about communists being poor. We always hear stories about communists starving to death."

Marat narrowed his eyes at Miles.

"*What?*" Miles said, holding out his hands. "It's just a joke."

Kevin gestured toward him. "He's a communist. You're joking about people like him starving to death."

Miles held up a finger. "*No*. No, no, no, no. I certainly wasn't making a joke about people starving to death."

"Dark stuff," Kevin repeated with a shake of his head.

Miles scoffed. "You want dark, I'll tell you a joke about a prostitute and a one-legged drunk." Miles pointed at his eyes. "Ends in tears, mate."

"My joke time." Marat hissed. "What do you call American with large penis?" Marat threw up his arms. "I don't know. No such thing exists."

Miles made a face. "That supposed to take the piss out of me, mate? I'm not a bloody American. Talk all the shit about the Yanks that you want. I'm British and he's Australian."

"*What do you call British with large penis?*" Marat went on.

"Loses a bit of the punch after you've fucked up, comrade." Miles shrugged.

Kevin went on, "I'm just saying. Couldn't tell a nice dick joke, you just had to make one about communists to a guy that just fled the Soviet Union? Bit insensitive is all."

"*I don't know. No such thing exists,*" Marat finished.

Miles held his hands up in surrender. "All right, all right, enough! Listen, Marat, I apologize, I meant no offense. I'm just a little on edge right now because I'm about to walk into the Oval Office and tell the president of the United States that the only way he can detect these alien bastards is to look and see if they have a cock or not. So if I—"

The door opened, interrupting Miles.

A secretary stuck her head out. "The president will see you now."

Miles glared at Kevin. "Still want that dick joke, or you ready to put your game face on?"

"Yeah, yeah, yeah." Kevin held up a hand in defeat as he stood up.

The secretary gave him an awkward look before leading the three in.

"No hard feelings, right mate?" Miles said and patted Marat on the back of the arm.

Marat shrunk back but nodded his head.

Miles lined up last and when no one was looking, rubbed his tired eyes.

Oh, what he wouldn't give for a drink right now, and my God, did he have to piss. That was just the nerves, though, because he'd already taken care of that business. Trick of the mind and all that.

Kevin and Marat walked forward without so much as a glance at the walls, but Miles couldn't help but look.

All the carpet, paintings, and statues—there was so much history here it could choke a man. He saw a bust of Abraham Lincoln with eyes that seemed to follow him. Miles glanced at it and then to Kevin. He pointed a finger at Lincoln, but Kevin, the bastard, hadn't even noticed.

Sure, sure, Miles had been in palaces before. He'd also been in drug dens, and caves, and worse, but for some damn reason, it was the White House that was giving him the jitters.

Because you shouldn't be here.

Ahh hell, that was the voice that liked to take a bite out of him.

You're a phony.

Well he'd always known that, nothing new there. He'd made a living out of it.

But this time you're going to get people killed.

He stopped suddenly, and the group continued.

"I, uhh—" Miles said beneath his breath as he rubbed the back of his head.

Miles was a lot of things.

An entertainer.

A con man.

An asshole.

But he wasn't this.

That same little curl of doubt that stretched and crawled was working its way into his stomach. He'd had that with his ex-wife, Shailene, right before things fell apart.

Right when he walked out.

Because the truth was, Miles Westwood wasn't a good man. He wasn't much of a man at all.

He was just good at making people think he was.

Miles spun on his heels, but a hand snatched him around the arm.

"Come on," Kevin said. "I'm not going to go in there without you and tell the president he has to tell everyone to get their pricks out."

"Mate, I'm not supposed to be here."

"And I am?"

"*Yeah*, you're the one that got vid of what the Soviets were doing in the bunker. You were the one that wanted to tell the world, you were the one that wrote that notebook. But me?" Miles pointed at his chest. "I'm just in for the money."

"That's not true, now *stop being an asshole* and let's go." Kevin grabbed Miles by the arm and tugged.

Miles took a step forward, half led by Kevin.

The secretary had the door to the Oval Office open and Marat waited to the side.

Somehow Miles ended up in front and stepped into the office first. President John Winters was there behind his desk, reading a datapad.

"Sir," the secretary said from behind Miles. "These are the experts the Soviet Union sent us."

John Winters looked up and sat his datapad down. "Good to meet you." He stood up and Miles was taken back by how tall and wide his shoulders were, like some stone statue of a man. "Gentlemen, I've been reading this report from the Soviets." He tapped the datapad. "And what I'm reading is fairly disturbing, but I'm not sure I understand what they're recommending."

"Sir," Miles said, and took a step forward. His mouth kept going even as his brain told it to stop. "It's true." He took a deep breath.

"You're going to have to tell everyone to get their nasty bits out."

TWENTY MINUTES into their meeting in the Oval Office, and they'd apparently piqued President Winters' interest, because he moved them into a meeting room that was never glamorous enough to be in any of the pictures, but Marat preferred it over the stature of the Oval Office with a picture of George Washington staring down every time he scratched his ass.

It was far more relaxed. President Winters had even taken off his jacket and rolled his sleeves up, and Marat bummed a cigarette off the secretary.

He had the smoldering cigarette in hand now.

The Englishman, Miles, was talking, and oh, was that bastard annoying. He grinned and moved his hands as he talked about some train that was covered in flesh and screamed.

Marat had seen the same damn thing, so he didn't feel the need to focus.

But somehow he still did—not on what he was saying, but *how* he said it.

If anything, Marat felt like he was getting worse at English.

He'd gone first when they got into the room. The president asked him about the gate and Marat explained what kind of research he did and how the gate withstood a nuclear strike, and kept functioning even when the power was cut. Marat pointed out that he had no idea how it remained functioning. "Maybe energy transfers from other side, but science says that is impossible."

The Englishman had made a face. "It was still functioning even when the power was cut? I thought wireless energy transfer was impossible?"

Marat had stared. Was the man fucking with him? He glanced around the room, but everyone watched as if awaiting Marat's response. An urge to scream—*That's what I said idiot*—had bubbled up Marat's throat, but he bit it down.

"Yes. Maybe impossible."

There it was. They understood him then. Maybe the key was stringing only a handful of words together? Any more than that, and apparently no one knew what he was talking about. It hadn't always been this bad, had it? Maybe he really was getting worse.

Marat was still contemplating that when the Australian—Marat thought his name was Kevin—explained that all that was needed for power transfer was a physical connection.

They had to suppose the gate itself was doing it then.

Somehow the energy was coming through the gate and powering the controls on their side.

That pretty much exhausted what Marat had to offer in the conversation.

None of these dumb bastards knew how smart he *really* was, but no, that wasn't the most tiresome part.

It was still the Englishman.

The man was grinning again right now as he made a *smoothing* gesture and talked about how the monsters didn't have any genitals.

No, by the way that bastard was smiling, Marat could tell he wasn't stressed at all.

And he'd been smiling the same way at Moller.

That really goaded Marat. When they first met, Marat watched as the Englishman's eyes slid up and down Moller like a wet tongue.

Oh, the thought of it right now made Marat squeeze his cigarette a little too hard and crush the damn thing.

Kevin gave him an awkward look and Marat stuffed it into an ashtray as if that was his plan the whole time, but all that did was make him even *more* irritated as he didn't have anything to smoke anymore.

"How was it?" President Winters asked.

Marat realized then that the whole room was looking at him.

"Hmm?" Marat narrowed his eyes.

The president cleared his throat. "Communication with the Chinese and the Iranians as they made their gates. We don't know much about it. Were they the same design?"

"Similar designs, but the work was constipated," Marat said.

They all stared at him confused.

Dammit, was something lost in translation again? Was his accent too thick?

"Work was constipated," he repeated slowly.

"Communications were difficult and unclear, that what you mean, mate?" the Englishman asked.

"Yes. Very difficult. Similar designs, but some differences," Marat agreed.

Oh, it had to be that bastard didn't it? He had to be the one to correct Marat in front of everyone.

Marat sank back into his chair as they all continued talking. Now he wished he had a damn dictionary in hand so he could look up the word constipated, because he was sure he'd studied that vocabulary word in school and had it right. He could even remember the exact wording in his textbook as clear as day.

Constipated: slow-moving or immobilized by overregulation.

There was a tap at the door and the secretary put her head in. "Mr. President, your wife is here."

John Winters nodded. "Gentlemen, I've found this to be more valuable than I could have hoped. I want to keep the three of you around for guidance. We'll have you set up nearby." With that, John stood up and left, and then the room was quiet.

Marat stared at the smoldering cigarette and tried to think where he could get another when the Englishman spoke.

"Well comrade, looks like we're a team from now on."

Marat lifted his chin with little enthusiasm. "Mmhmm."

"And mate." The Englishman flashed his annoying grin. "Let me explain to you how we use the word *constipated*."

15

ZHAO SAT at a table fourteen floors below ground in a bunker dubbed *Heaven's Gate*. It was an immense and expensive bunker inherited from the previous regime.

That old ruler, the one thrown from the roof of his own palace, had a habit of giving everything a name of divine nature.

Zhao did not.

A committee had been formed to rename it just the year before, but nothing seemed to fit. A *Heaven's Gate* buried under several million pounds of dirt never made much sense to Zhao.

Hell's Doorstep would have been more suitable.

Zhao sat at the end of a long marble table. Empty chairs lined the sides, but rotating screens sat directly above them. All the governors of the twenty-two provinces of China were in virtual attendance, and their faces filled the screens.

The governors were hard, stone-faced individuals who had clawed their way into their position. Not one of them had inherited power, no, all of that had gone the way of the grave when the old powers were dismantled in revolution, and the old leader of China thrown to a screaming death.

These were people that understood the scent of weakness and the utility of violence.

Some came dressed with modest black suits and ties like Zhao. Others were in traditional garb, and even one governess had her hair done up in an elaborate, cultural fashion of centuries past.

It was important that when Zhao addressed them, he stood firmly as one in control.

To show weakness was to invite a challenge, even in these desperate times.

Zhao believed that most were loyal, but there may be a wolf or two among them.

Surely someone was waiting to try their own hand at party leadership.

The only person in the room other than the staff was Wu, and though the man usually smoked or lounged, today he sat up straight and to the right of Zhao.

He, too, understood the appearance of weakness and disobedience.

Zhao leaned forward on the table with his hands clasped together.

"Play the vid," Zhao ordered.

A large screen on the wall lit up, but Zhao didn't watch it. He focused on the faces of the governors.

A grainy black and white vid taken from high orbital cameras showed a woman in armor walking among a horde of beasts.

Alice Winters.

Large, bulbous creatures, waddled up on massive legs and surrounded her, their flesh tightening around her body.

The camera immediately cut off as a missile strike hit near her position faster than the eye could see. It threw waste and toxic particles in the air, making it impossible for the camera to see anything else.

"End vid," Zhao said, and the screen darkened. "Play scouting log one forty-seven."

The screen immediately turned to a view directly from a soldier's helmet. It jumped and bobbed with the soldier's movement, and there was static popping on the screen, the result of radiation. Other squad members moved alongside the man, and above them, yellow irradiated clouds swirled in unnatural ways, lightning cracking within them, and gray toxins leaked up from the soil.

There was no sound as the soldier stopped and scanned across an empty field that looked to be filled with countless open graves—holes dug deep into the dirt. Just at a glance, Zhao could see there were easily thousands.

The soldier kept looking over the field until he saw a large mound. He pointed at it and glanced toward the soldiers at his side.

"Freeze," Zhao said. "Forward to the next vid mark."

The screen flashed and now the mound was only a few feet away and the soldier's hand was outstretched and frozen on the paused vid. The mound had strange brown and black layers cutting across each other with thick, grooved lines like veins.

There were faces and arms of monsters fused into the side.

"Play."

The soldier's hand moved and it touched the mound. The camera scanned over the thick shell and then back to see the other soldiers with their rifles trained forward. The vid passed over a spot where it looked like the mouth of a cronux had melted into it.

The soldier moved around the mound until he saw a hole within the fused flesh. It was higher than the camera could easily look into, so the soldier turned and tossed his rifle to another and grabbed the edges, one hand fitted into an open jaw for a hold.

He grabbed onto the edge of the hole and hoisted up.

There was wilted grass inside. The radiation had poisoned it.

But the soldier turned to look back on the ground.

The grass was missing everywhere else—fried up in the initial strike.

The mound had protected whatever was inside.

"Wu, inform the governors what the analyst concluded," Zhao said.

The spymaster cleared his throat and then stood at attention, placing his hands behind his back. His gold-framed glasses sat low on his nose.

"Our intelligence analysts believe this was a cocoon, one formed around Alice Winters. It seems."

A look of confusion spread across some of the faces there.

"The Americans did this?" an old, bald governor with a gray beard asked.

"That much is unclear," Wu said, his chin uncharacteristically tipped up. "But you all have seen the video. For whatever the reasons are, she is now leading forces against us. You all saw the video she made. She tried to release that to the population, but we were able to intercept it."

"What was the aim in delivering the message to the population?" the bald governor asked.

"Panic. Disorder," Zhao answered. "If the people can put a face to the monsters, then the fear will spread deeper and more quickly. Under my orders, we have suppressed the video, and our disinformation teams have produced counterfeit copies that were supplied to the media to analyze as fake in case there is any leak. Needless to say, we must keep this quiet."

The bald governor nodded his head, and Wu pointed at the screen and made a bit of a face as he searched for a word. "Her *travel companions* were some of the same that were in Moscow when it was nuked. We believe the species is adapting. They have institutional memory for what has happened to them, and apparently they took precautions before the strike. They burrowed into the ground before the missile struck. That alone shouldn't have been enough to save them, so we have to assume that there are other evolved characteristics. But the cocoon around Alice Winters was apparently made of the fused bodies of some of the underlings, and it may indicate that their flesh is resistant to the intense heat generated. Essentially the missile strike did little except make a portion of Xinjiang uninhabitable and created nuclear winds that will threaten nearby regions." Wu tsked his lips, but still looked only mildly annoyed at best. "Unfortunate."

Zhao could see the Xinjiang governor's face. A young man in his early forties.

His face was tightened in anger and disgust at the poisoning of his province. "I was not informed a missile would land within my territory."

"There was little time to act, it needed to be done quickly," Wu answered.

"Quick enough that they had time to burrow within the ground?" the governor scoffed.

"They are remarkable diggers apparently. It must have been done quickly." Wu tilted his head ever so slightly. "Something to be noted."

The Xinjiang governor puffed up his cheeks. "Our exterior cities have already reported the horde. This enemy is no longer baying at the gate, they are within, and they are killing my people."

"*Our people*," Zhao said. There were a few moments of silence as Zhao stared at the screen.

The governor finally bowed his head. "Of course, Chairman, I only wish to know what the party intends to do on this growing threat. Will there be further nuclear strikes?"

Zhao glanced toward Wu to give the answer.

"There will be no further strikes. The first proved useless, and more damaging to us than to them. The only effective use would be one with negative impact capabilities to penetrate deep, but we would permanently damage our water sources. They will only be used as a last resort."

"Yes, *a last resort*," the governess of Gansu said, her hair drawn tight and her makeup immaculate. "In defense of Beijing and the heart of the government, but not for those of us in the outer provinces. The Soviets were unable to stand against this enemy, and Europe is reeling. Only the Americans have yet to see it spread, but their time will come I am sure."

"*Enough*," Zhao hissed. "I did not call a meeting of leadership to engage in fear and trembling. Gansu, as is Xinjiang, are all part of Chinese soil. We will take back every bit of dirt, but we will do so as a whole."

"Chairman," the governor of Tibet called out, a stone-faced man in glasses. "The enemy has engaged our garrisons, and we have sustained heavy losses, but we repelled them each time. Our people are strong. We will stand guard for China. They will not break us."

"But they will. They will break us if we squabble, and separate ourselves." Zhao rose from his seat. "This is why I'm ordering each of you to conduct an eighth directive scale military draft. We will form the largest army China and the world has ever seen. We will stand united in the face of this enemy. No province, no city, no mound of dirt will remain uncontested. We will water the soil with the blood of patriots until the enemy is defeated, and we will show the world that China does not bow."

The Taiwan governess, dressed in a traditional white gown with red trimming, bowed her head before speaking. "We will begin immediately. Taiwan will offer all that she has to the cause, but may I humbly ask a question of you, Chairman?" She raised her head now to meet Zhao's eyes. "Where is the Dragon?"

Her words silenced the room.

Zhao's hands tightened their grip.

His face remained stiff.

"You were all provided with intelligence. The Dragon has become overwhelmed by madness, and the Dragonskin program has shut down."

"But Chairman," another governor said with a frown. "We will all send our sons and daughters to war in defense of China, but we would like to know what steps are being taken to reactivate the program and to bring the Dragon back into service."

"This, too, was on the order of business to be discussed today." Zhao looked at the screen. "Play vid fourteen thirty-six."

The governors watched in silence as a camera feed played. It was a video from inside the gymnasium where the Dragonskin program was conducted.

All was calm, but there was movement. Plastic sheets were set up between beds and volunteers were being wheeled in and out on gurneys while technicians exposed them to parasites harvested from the horde that now remained in Mongolia.

There was blood and death, but there was order. Flame troopers walked down the line, the tips of their weapons hissing fire, prepared to kill.

In one corner, there was a panic as something got loose.

Zhao kept his eyes on the screen. To do anything else would be noticed. Everything he said or did was noted by those around him.

Zhao was more than a man—he was the symbol of China's greatness—and he could not show fear or weakness, lest he invite a challenge from another.

The chaos in the video began to spread but the flame soldiers let loose with heat and scorched the infected. Black smoke rolled up into the air, and the camera began to lose focus.

And all would have been brought under control if not for the Dragon.

He entered the gymnasium, and he walked differently than ever before, not with his back straight but arched over with his fingers curled like claws. The large metallic dome on his head was unmistakable, and the mechanical arm waved up on one side like a viper ready to strike.

The infected rushed past him without so much as bumping his side.

The vid feed was silent but creatures' mouths were open, expressing horrible howls.

The flame soldiers turned and let loose with more fire and cooked the oncoming attacks.

The Dragon took no notice as he continued in, his bare feet on the cold ground.

Bare feet. That was something that Zhao always noticed, somehow that stood out to him for one reason or another. The strangeness was that the Dragon would choose to walk barefoot outside.

But why would that matter? The Dragon was engaged in a fit of madness rage.

But for the Chinese, it was custom to remove shoes only when entering the house, and even then, they often put on slippers.

Zhao could not remember a time where he had walked barefoot outside. Such a thing was unheard of in China.

But the Dragon was not Chinese.

That realization settled into Zhao's stomach.

Of course he knew who the Dragon was, and that he was not Han Chinese.

No. It wasn't that he wasn't Han Chinese.

He wasn't Chinese at all.

He was Kasher.

On the vid, most of the flame soldiers were overwhelmed and only one remained, backed into a corner, still blasting the air with fire. More smoke rolled up and the camera lost focus.

The vid stopped.

There was silence as the governors all glanced up on their screens, the vid ending for them.

All eyes were once more upon Zhao.

"The Dragon seized the building. All cameras inside have been disabled. The windows have been blocked by the charred bodies of the dead. We have the building cordoned off, and we are working to improve the situation."

"Chairman, your excellent leadership and calculations gave us the Dragon and helped quell the initial exposures of the gate in Beijing," one governor said, an older man with slicked back hair and an unpleasant smile. "With your wisdom and guidance, we will surely succeed, but I would also like clarifications. I have heard that a team was sent into the building where the Dragon is now."

"Yes," Zhao said, his voice flat.

"And that they did not return?"

"This is true."

"And, Mr. Chairman, many of us do not have the fortitude and forbearance that you have been gifted with. Could you calm our worries by telling us what will be done to reengage the Dragon?"

Zhao stared at the man and the man stared back.

All others watched.

"We have the resources to begin the Dragonskin program again, and we will do so immediately. The Dragon will be dealt with, quickly, and sent back into the field. This will be a top priority of my office."

"Thank you, Mr. Chairman, my worries and concerns are calmed." The governor did not bow his head, but kept eye contact the entire time he spoke.

Zhao turned to face the others. "The details of the military draft will be sent to you soon, and you will be given transportation instructions soon. Logistics are already in movement to support the oncoming draft. We are adjourned."

Each governor bowed their head.

The governor of Hubei was the last to do so.

Each video went black.

Wu lounged back into his chair. "How unwise of the governor of Hubei to tip his hand so clearly."

Zhao shook his head. "By doing so he sent the others a message. He expects to be next in line should I be replaced."

"He had a son die in combat in the defense of Beijing. Perhaps it's more personal than professional."

"I would never separate those two things."

"You are correct." Wu adjusted his glasses and fished a cigarette from his pocket. "Chairman, may I speak bluntly?" He put it into his mouth and brought out an electric lighter.

Zhao watched with mild irritation as Wu lit the cigarette. "The only reason I accept your constant disrespect is because you are one of the few that will."

"We'll lose this war without the Dragon." Wu took a drag. "We may place our formidable army between us and them, but all we will do is buy time. We must reacquire him. Violently if need be."

"Indeed, he is necessary." Zhao moved back into his seat and leaned forward to clasp his hands together. "It's not often that I get news before you."

"Hmm?" Wu made a curious face.

Zhao looked back to the screen. "Play local transmission sixty-four at designation mark. Sound on."

The screen flashed on and Wu looked toward it.

It was another video feed from a soldier's helmet; in the corner of the screen, there were indicators that identified the vid as Duty Officer Suen. It was nearing sunset and the gloom casted shadows across the city. The vid picked up mid sentence, "—*settling the night guard and*—"

"*Sir!*" someone shouted.

The feed turned toward the entrance of the building where something came shuffling out. There were no arms on the naked corpse, and the flesh was so burned it was impossible to tell who it was.

"*Is that the Dragon? Do we fire?*" someone asked.

"*Negative, hold!*" It was Suen's voice. "*Halt, halt!*" The soldiers aimed their rifles.

The creature hissed out words, but the soldiers shouting made it impossible to hear.

"*What's it saying? I can't hear it.*"

"*Do we fire? Do we fire?*"

"*Negative!*" Suen commanded again.

The corpse collapsed to its knees and tilted its head back and shouted, but it was still impossible to hear over the soldiers.

"*Quiet!*" Suen ordered. "*Everyone quiet!*"

The creature howled, throwing its head back again.

"*Sir, I have a clear shot!*"

"*No further incoming hostiles!*"

"*I said quiet dammit!*" Suen ordered, and he must have adjusted the dial on his helmet because it zoomed in.

Zhao could practically smell the man's charred flesh. He'd smelled it back in the old days of the revolt, and it was a scent few would forget.

The corpse's arms were removed and its lips were shriveled.

"*Zhao!*" it called out. "*Send Zhao!*"

"End vid," Zhao said, and looked to Wu. "That transmission was sent to me twenty minutes before this meeting began."

Wu looked unnerved, he wasn't lounging in his seat, but almost shrinking into it. "That was highly unpleasant." Wu held his cigarette. "What are your intentions?"

Zhao tilted his head. "To go and speak with him."

Wu froze in place for a moment. "Chairman, that would be foolish. Perhaps he only wants to get you close so that he could kill you."

"I suspect not. But perhaps. No one is too valuable to lose. If I'm killed then you will serve my successor, but I feel that the Dragon intends to negotiate."

Wu took the cigarette from his mouth and leaned back into his chair, his eyes on Zhao. "Why do you suspect that?"

Zhao looked back to the screen. "Play local transmission thirty-four at the third designation mark." It was a video of the gymnasium. There were a few moments of calm before the Dragon showed up, and the infected followed alongside him as they entered into the building. Zhao made a gesture toward it. "Because the first thing he did was kill our leverage."

16

MOLLER STEPPED up onto a systems platform, and two teams of techs rolled her metal cases over. She unbuttoned her jacket and tossed it aside. She undid her belt and pulled her pants off, dressing down to her skin suit—a black synthetic weave with white lines of circuitry across it.

"This is some dumb shit," Major Evans, Moller's liaison, said with a pinch of tobacco under his lip.

"Which part?" Moller smoothed her sleeves down to the wrist on both arms.

"The part where it's happening. Have you ever done a high altitude drop before?"

"I've done drops before."

"I said a *high altitude* drop. It's not the same thing." He spit into the corner of the floor, eliciting a bad look from a tech that was preparing the armor. "We don't have the accuracy and this rig is untested anyway. You might smack into a building."

"That's why we're aiming for open beach. It has to be that way. If we went lower, we'd risk having the ship downed."

"How the hell can those things hit aircraft?" Evans asked.

Moller turned to face Evans and tied her hair back as she spoke.

"They've adapted. Large things that look like walking tumors can somehow launch themselves into the trajectory of a plane and take them out. I've seen the vids."

"I have too, but it's still hard to believe. Where are you going to go?"

She finished tying her hair up and stepped off the platform. She grabbed her datapad off a counter and handed it to him.

Evans looked down to see a blue digital map of Long Island, with a series of expanding green circles with X's in various locations. "See that? That's where every breakout has been. There's an epicenter in the middle. They're smart, but they're not that smart. It's all unfolding from the center there in Long Island."

Evans glowered at the map. "What the hell are you going to do there?"

"I already told you. I'm going to go see what's in that epicenter."

Evans tossed the datapad back onto the counter. "What are you hoping to find?"

"I don't know yet. But whatever it is, it'll be something terrible."

Evans rubbed his chin. "We're going to be attacking here in the next few days. We're getting everything in position and all the civilians out to make a clean sweep of it, so why even risk dying?"

Moller looked toward the techs and asked, "Almost done?"

One of them gave her a thumbs-up. "Five more minutes. We're calibrating the health systems."

She looked back at Evans and pointed to the armor. "That's experimental irradiated armor. We noticed in Russia that it blocked the hive mind's connection, and we theorized that it'll help me evade them."

"Has it been used before?"

"No, I'll be testing."

Evans snorted. "Rolling the dice on your life then, aren't you?"

Moller let out a breath. "I am and I'm willing to. I knew someone who got sucked in through one of their gates. That was years ago."

"Years ago?" Evans frowned. Felicity was still classified, but Moller didn't care anymore. It didn't matter.

"Yes. His name was Cameron Elliot. Now do you know what I saw in the Soviet Union when I was there? Something coming through the gate that had a face just like his. Just like Cameron Elliot's."

That quieted Evans. He watched her, unsure of what to say.

"I don't know how many people went through that gate, or if they even had Cameron, but if I had to guess, they took him in and they've been poking around in his body learning about us ever since. They know a lot more about us than we do about them. I don't have any idea what's in that epicenter, but I know I want to find out before they unleash it."

Evans took a sharp breath. "You've got some balls for a girl with a ponytail."

A technician called over, "Agent Moller, we're checked and ready to go. We'll need to clear the room."

Moller motioned for Evans to leave. "Be safe, Major."

Evans back stepped. "You know the world's ending right? If you make it out, how about you let me buy you a drink?"

That actually gave her a grin. "Be safe, Major," she repeated.

"I know the boys that do drops. I'm going to see if I can hitch a ride. Just to make sure you don't get into any trouble." He grinned and headed out the door.

Technicians in hazmat suits closed the door and sealed it with a pop.

Teams pushed the metal cases over to her while a datascreen to the side revealed the toxicity level. A technician came to stand in front of her, his voice buzzing from a speaker set into his mask. "Arms out to your side please." He spread his arms to guide her. The other technicians took pieces of the armor out with loud snaps. With his arms still to his side the tech instructed her, "Be careful with this. If there's any major breach, you could be exposed to the radiation. It's low yield, and you'll have the under suit, but I wouldn't want to sit in it. It's why we have to be so cautious."

"Understood," she said.

The technician nodded then grabbed a face mask off the container. He fitted it over her head. The plastic lenses fogged up as Moller breathed and the tech fastened it in place.

"The CAG systems will even things out and get rid of that fog when the helmet is on." The tech gave her a thumbs-up. Two other techs fitted gloves onto her hands and used straps to bring them up to her shoulders."

Moller steadied her breathing as the lenses fogged to the point where she couldn't see anything, just blurry images as the techs pulled pieces out of the suit.

They dug out the boots and motioned for her to raise each foot and strapped the pieces on. Maybe it was just in her head, but she felt an electric buzz as each piece snapped into place.

A team came over and fitted the leg armor, using tools that looked like specialized drills to form the armor to her proportions.

Three techs came over carrying the chest piece and connected it onto the waist joints. It gave a loud magnetic *click* as it locked. Another group brought over the back shield and slid it in with the same loud *click*.

Two technicians in front of her worked her chest plate into position, and fitted it into a connection. As they pressed it up to the back joints, internal locks connected and the armor gave a series of satisfied chirps.

The team with the drills worked the tools into small inlets and wound the armor down in pieces to fit her shape.

Moller tried to steady her breathing but the fog on her lenses was making her anxious. She twisted her neck some and the face mask rubbed against her skin, making her feel incredibly claustrophobic.

They buckled on arm joints as she held stiff.

"Space your fingers, please," one of the techs said and slid the oversized gloves on. They brought up the drill into a joint and drilled the armor gloves down snug to her hands.

Moller didn't yet have her helmet on, only the mask, but a technician walked in front of her and called, "Follow me please." He motioned his arms out and Moller followed. He stood on one foot and then the other, and she mirrored it. He flexed his arms up and turned at the waist. She did the same. He gave a small hop and Moller followed, though she barely moved from the ground at all.

"Recalibrate strength ratings," the technician called over to a member on a computer. Long black cables ran from his station to somewhere in the back of Moller's armor.

The computer technicians clicked keys together and gave a thumbs-up.

The technician in front of her motioned to focus on him again. "Follow me once more." He went down low and hopped into the air six inches above the ground.

Moller leaned down and jumped, she went two feet into the air and came down with a hard thud.

The technician gave her a thumbs-up. "A little higher than I'd like, but that might be the best we can do with this prototype system. Be careful with the sensitivity of your movements."

Moller held up a thumb.

The tech at the computer module gave a thumbs-up. "All systems go. Life support functions running on optimal patterns. Combat system logistics are optimized."

The tech in front of Moller gave a thumbs-up back toward the computer then stepped up closer to her. "The systems here are different from your normal CAG. Everything will lock in place and take a minute or two to click on while the system runs diagnostics on itself before activating, so don't panic."

She nodded and he slowly set the helmet down on Moller, and twisted it into the right position before it settled onto her shoulders.

Everything went dark and the armor tightened.

She couldn't move.

Moller took a deep breath in and out. In and out.

It was a tomb. She couldn't hear anything from the outside and it was pitch black.

Her own breathing sounded much louder than it should, and it was quite uncomfortable, but she'd been through worse.

Three by three . . .

That thought came in and it caught her so fast she stopped breathing.

And nothing more . . .

It was Eli's tune. And in her head she could hear it with the same little *nails-on-the-chalkboard* voice.

One to none, and then the fun.

She'd never heard that rhyme before. He must have made it himself.

Why the hell would a kid say something so disturbing?

Break the back and eat the dead...

The King will laugh but has no head...

She thought a lot about him. She remembered how he sat down, his back to her, and twisted his head so far to look at her she thought it might pop off.

The party then is such a bore...

She honestly thought he might be insane. She'd said as much to Roles.

So now we say, three by three and nothing more.

But he'd told her that Alice was still alive and she was with the Archon.

Moller didn't know if she believed that, but when she asked Eli who he'd been talking to, he told her.

The one in New York.

All at once, the internal lighting came on and a visual screen popped up. The CAG loosened now and she could move.

She waved a hand in front of her face, but it was still blurry. She glanced around the room, but her vision was even worse than before. She pointed at her helmet screen and cut her hand through the air.

A voice buzzed onto her comms.

"Give the systems a moment to clear up the visual impairments."

She waited until there was the sound like a fan coming on and a loud popping. Her mask tightened up against the inside of the helmet and the lenses cleared up.

The voice came once more, *"How's that? Have you gained visual clarity?"*

Moller waved her hand in front of her face again, but she could see everything now. She gave a thumbs-up. "Confirmed."

"Acknowledged."

A technician stepped in front of her again and motioned for her to walk down the platform.

Moller took several powerful steps down. The CAG was much stiffer than her old system. Much like a munitions disposal CAG, it wasn't intended for intense combat situations.

Moller only hoped it worked like they theorized.

The technicians motioned for her to stop and she halted at the base of the platform.

He tapped the side of his head, and Moller reached over to her gauntlet and adjusted the external speakers.

"Can you hear me?" the tech asked.

"Yes," she said.

"Let's do another rundown then. Your armor is irradiated, so we cannot let you near others for any prolonged period of time. The armor is double enforced and supposed to hide your presence. If you go stiff, they should overlook you, however, it's also going to be more difficult to move and fight, so try not to engage."

"I'll ask them politely to let me pass."

"Hey, if it works." The tech made a circle with his finger. *"You'll also have to adjust your filters when the readouts demand it. Can you place one in now?"*

Moller lifted her arm and found a notch in the left elbow of her CAG that was bulkier than the other side. She lifted a small hatch and there was a large empty port. She reached to her hip and dug out a filter that looked little more than an extra large battery. She plugged it in and her screen flashed green.

The technician watched as she made each step. *"Excellent. Now you'll need the power cells for boosted effects. You have a constant low yield, but these cells will flood the systems and make you shed increased radiation for a time. In theory it should help in situations with more sensitive entities. The whole process is highly dangerous though, so it's imperative that if your suit is compromised, or if there are friendlies around, you do not use the boost. Can you locate them in your elbow sheath?"*

Moller lifted up her arm and moved a hatch on the left elbow. There were eight thin cells that she could slide out.

"Good. No need to take one out now." He motioned for her to come forward. *"Now let's try to walk the room."*

Moller moved forward, and the CAG made a noise like a machine press with each step. She headed around the room in a circle before settling back into the center of the room.

The tech folded his arms behind his back.*"How do your systems read?"*

Moller looked at her digital gauges. In the top corner of her vision, there was a camera that showed her what was at her back.

"All systems green," she said.

"Then I think we're good to go." He pointed at the other techs. *"Bring it up."*

The two metal cases the CAG had traveled in were now locked together. The techs wheeled it over in front of Moller and snapped the tops.

He slapped the top of it with two loud thuds. *"We call it the tomb. Nothing like a little black humor, right?"*

MOLLER CLOSED her eyes and controlled her breathing.

In.

Out.

In.

Out.

There was a soft glow of light on her screen, but everything else was dark, and she could only hear soft thuds as she was loaded up onto a transport helicopter.

The irradiated armor had to be transported in a reinforced case to keep contamination to a minimum.

What that meant in effect was that Moller had to be transported in the tomb out to Long Island.

"How's it going in there?" Major Evan's voice buzzed into her helmet.

Moller opened her eyes and saw Evan's face. He was looking into a self-facing camera mounted on his headset.

"About as good as could be expected." She could see the outside window of the helicopter behind Evans and the clouds speeding behind it. "So you got the ride after all?"

He grinned *"You bet. I don't envy you, though, my last CAG training was over a weekend two years ago. I always hate not being able to scratch my ass. Can't imagine not being able to even move my arms. But hey, at least you have a few minutes to think about that drink with me, right?"* Evans glanced up at the camera and smirked before looking down at his computer module and typing commands.

"How far out are we?" she asked.

Evans looked down at his screen and clicked a few keys. *"Looks like twenty minutes until the drop. We've got some aircraft circling now and dropping flares to try and grab their attention before we dump you near the harbor."*

"The harbor? I thought we agreed to go further inland?"

"No can do. The pilot says the creatures are too heavy there. One could hit you midair, or we might end up launching you into a building. You're just going to have to hike it inland. We'll send you out five miles from the target location. When you're ready for pickup, you'll need to huff it back to the pod and hit the call signal. We'll have a team on standby."

"Confirmed."

Evans looked away again and clicked on his keyboard. *"We're coming up on the drop location. Anything I could do before we unload?"*

"Major, I'm locked up in the *tomb*, and like you said before, I can't scratch my own ass. What can you do for me?"

"Provide some inspiring conversation, and ask you again about that drink."

"That's the third time you've asked me, and I ignored you the first two."

"Third time's a charm, right?" He looked up at the screen and grinned.

"Ask me when I'm not about to go into a war zone."

"So fourth time's the charm then?"

"Maybe. Might have had better luck if I hadn't seen you spitting tobacco." She grinned. "Hey, Major? Thanks for helping me think of something else other than being in the *tomb.*"

He glanced toward the camera and gave a salute. *"That's what I'm here for."* There was a flash of red lighting up on Evan's face; he glanced down toward the computer.

"What's that?" she asked.

"Wait a moment." Evans started typing, and Moller could see his eyes darting across the screen. *"Seems like we're getting some system interference."* Evans put his hand to his ear and looked away, hearing something that Moller could not. He looked back. *"That was the pilot, he said we're aborting the mission. We're going to have to return. We just have to—"*

The pod rattled and her screen blanked.

"Major? *Major?*"

Moller took rapid breaths. She tried to move but was frozen in place.

The screen popped back on. Evans had moved, and now he was yelling. *"Moller, something just fried our systems, and we lost an engine! We're going to put you down now."*

"What's happening? Where will I land?"

There was a loud screech of metal that made Moller grind her teeth.

She felt the tomb slide out of the ship, and go into free fall. The armor held her in place, but she could feel her stomach rising like when she shot down a rollercoaster.

There was a sudden impact and the stabilizers kept her from the worst of the impact as her body shook.

Glowing words flashed across the screen.

Landing Error. Landing Error. Landing Error.

In a frenzy, she yanked at her hand, but it stayed in position.

Moller took more rapid breaths and kicked her legs, but all she did was push up against the padding.

A bead of sweat ran down her face and then turned and ran the other direction.

The tomb was turning end over end, but her sense of vertigo kept her from thinking clearly.

In a panic, Moller screamed and thrashed but nothing budged.

"Oh fuck!" she hissed out. "Oh God, oh God!" she was locked in and now her skin was crawling.

The crawl.

A condition noticed by users with prolonged use in CAG. The inability to move or wipe sweat away made the skin feel like it was going to crawl off.

It made some go insane.

"Help! Help!" She lost herself to a sense of madness. She tugged her arms and kicked her legs. She must have smashed her nose because it bled now. First down her lip and then up into her eye. She blinked hard as the blood ran over, and changed position to streak across her nose.

She was going to die unsure of what was even happening.

Alone in the tomb.

No, Moller said internally even as she kept gasping for breath.

You're not going to die.

Moller clamped down her teeth and stifled her breathing as she focused.

"Computer, bring up operational commands."

A digital screen came on, but it was hard to see with all the blood in her eyes, and even now, she kept reflexively feeling her arm shift to wipe it away.

"Enable audio reporting functions."

A dull male's voice came on, *"Audio functions enabled. How may I—"*

Moller interrupted. "Exterior diagnostics. Where have I landed?"

"Processing. Processing. Processing. Undetermined."

Moller hissed in frustration. "Breach hull."

There were two loud beeps. *"Negative. Hull breach while in motion does not meet safety standards."*

"Override!" she yelled. "Systems processing in error. Diagnostic functions unreliable, retract to operator judgment. *Breach the fucking hull!"*

"Processing. Processing. Processing. Confirmed."

There was a series of clicks as locks burst. The hull split open down the middle and spilled Moller out.

She shifted and swirled as air bubbles flowed past her.

She had landed in the water.

And she was sinking.

Moller waved her arms to swim, but the armor was too slow and heavy.

She sank down into the blackness of the water, the fading light on the surface growing ever distant.

The tomb casings still glowed and shined light into the water as they sank along with her.

Moller kicked and squirmed, but it was all useless.

Then she saw the shadow just outside the light.

A large snaking worm came flowing into the water. It was massive in size, and Moller's eyes lit up.

It had changed, but she'd seen that beast before. It was in Berlin.

Its face came to a point and the layers peeled back showing a wide mouth. It swallowed one of the lids from the tomb and kept swimming by.

Moller turned and swung her arms but it still did nothing.

It only grabbed the attention of the worm.

"Oh fuck, oh fuck!" Moller panicked as she faced it and waved her arms back.

The worm came swimming toward her, its mouth peeling open. The tomb lid half inside its throat still glowed and illuminated its tendrils rolling out to reach for Moller.

She swung her arms back and forth and hit the back of her hand on the tomb lid. She grabbed onto it and pulled it around.

The worm went to swallow her and she shoved the lid in. The tendrils came up wrapping over it and grabbing onto her arm as it pulled her in.

Moller drew into its throat, and its lips peeled down over her as she sank into its gut; she saw its pink insides with thousands of pointed notches grabbed and shredded everything entering its mouth.

One tendril wrapped up around her leg and gave her a tug.

Moller clung to the lid like a life raft and screamed as she was swallowed alive.

She saw the computer screen inside the tomb with large visible words on it.

Processing. Processing. Processing.

Then she saw her rifle, still locked in place within the tomb.

She grabbed the butt of the rifle, and thumped the bottom of her hand on the release button.

The rifle came loose and she tightened it into her grip and turned toward the fleshy center of the worm.

She pulled the trigger and saw a burst of air bubbles.

Thump-thump-thump-thump-thump.

The worm's insides shook as flaps of skin popped and inky-black blood spilled into the water. The worm reacted by tightening its bite, but only crushed down on the tomb.

It then whipped its head back and forth, but Moller kept squeezing the trigger.

In a violent gag, the worm spit her and the tomb lid out.

The large lid sank, but Moller grabbed onto a thick, white whisker on the worm's face and climbed across it.

In a mad fury, the worm bit at the lid again as Moller climbed across its face, fitting her hand into the pits and grooves of the worm's flesh.

With a sudden burst, the creature moved and Moller lost hold. A fin went by and she grabbed onto it. The creature sped through the water with Moller clinging to it. She fit her rifle strap around one arm and let it go loose as she hung on.

The worm went up and down at incredible speeds, and even in the armor Moller felt like she might lose consciousness. It took a drastic U-turn, and Moller was hurled off it.

She went back first into the deep, her hands reaching up toward the fading light of the surface.

Then she smacked the bottom. It was too dark to see anything, but she felt her hand easily press into the ground. She clicked the switch for her head lamp and a light on top of her helmet came on, illuminating the ground. She looked around and saw a large concrete wall. She shuffled toward it and ran her hand over it. There were grooves big enough to fit her hands in. Moller looked back. If the worm came down, she'd be exposed, but there was no other choice. She fit her boot into a notch and climbed the wall.

She went up and she could see light through the murky water. Another bead of sweat dripped down her face and Moller blinked hard. She started again and didn't stop until she broke the surface. Everything in her wanted to gasp for breath, but that was entirely unnecessary. There was another twenty feet of concrete and now she needed to stop each time and base her fist into it to get a good hold.

She finally got one hand up to the surface and was able to grab a fixed metal post. She held onto that and pulled the rest of the way up until she could crawl over. She stayed down and rolled onto her back to stare up at the sky. There was black smoke, but she was too tired to care at the moment.

She lay there for a few minutes before turning back over. She looked up and down the small section of the harbor.

She saw the dropship.

It had crashed and skidded across the road. She could see the groves in the torn asphalt.

It was swarmed by the infected. They were so thick she could only see what was over their heads.

She rotated a dial on her helmet, and her screen zoomed in.

There was smoke, but it didn't look like it had been hit. There weren't the blast marks like she'd seen on the others that were targeted by cronux.

This looked like it had just fallen out of the air.

Moller took one step in that direction but froze.

The hull door was broken in.

The creatures were inside.

Everyone was dead.

With a sigh she turned away. She hoped Major Evans had gone quickly.

She took her rifle off her shoulder and checked it. Water had seeped in and likely carried dirt and sand. With another glance around, she took aim at the water and pulled the trigger.

Thick.

The gun made a useless click. It was jammed, and she couldn't clear it. Not without tools and in these gloves.

Useless.

With one last look to the dropship, she dropped the rifle on the ground and turned toward the city.

The gun didn't work, but she still had work to do.

17

THREE LEVELS BELOW GROUND, there was no daylight, but there were still strong smells.

Piss and blood.

It was here even in the control hub for the local subway cars. There had been another control that sat on the surface before, but authorities had built this one below ground.

It doubled as a shelter for war.

The Janissary knew this because the manager had known it, and the Janissary had just eaten his brain.

The Janissary's long fingers were still wet and covered with chunks.

He licked the oil off his fingers with a long, gray tongue.

"Please," pleaded another man, flat on his ass and hiding behind a chair.

The Janissary glanced in his direction and licked a chunk off another finger.

Please. What did that word mean?

The Janissary dug his nails into the open skull in his lap and heaved another handful into his mouth.

Electric sparks popped inside the Janissary. Flashes of incomplete knowledge. Much was gained, but most was lost.

It only meant that the process had to be repeated over and over to gain a fuller picture.

The Janissary pushed the dead man aside and he thudded against the ground. His corpse left to join the pile on the floor.

"No, no!" The man tucked his head into his arm.

It was strange that this place had been built for defense. All it really did was gather them all into one place.

When the Janissary broke the walls and went inside, there was no hope for anyone within.

They were all dead within minutes.

How many had there been? Hundreds? Maybe thousands?

The Janissary cared little for those details. The only reason he considered it at all was because it was part of the flash of knowledge within his mind. An incomplete number, that was useless nonetheless.

There were other facts and tidbits that the Janissary considered.

Dates. Car models. Sex. Politics.

Useless.

Infrastructure. Geography. Weapons. Technology.

These are what he wanted to know.

He licked another thick chunk off his finger and stood up, his body taller than any man. Fins on the side of his head flashed open, displaying a blood red flesh patch as he walked over to the man on the ground. The Janissary grabbed the chair and pulled it aside as the man blubbered. There was no real struggle, the Janissary simply reached down and grabbed the man by the arm and lifted him into the air.

Then bit into his head.

Now the man thrashed and fought, but the Janissary dug his fingers into the wound and opened the rest of the skull up like a soup can. The Janissary scooped out and sucked down the wet chunks.

There were bright flashes in his mind now. There always were with the first few bites.

A computer system network unfolded within his thoughts.

This man had been a computer technician here.

The Janissary took another bite and more flashes came to him.

He saw it.

Thump.

The body had slipped from his grasp, and now its brains leaked out onto the floor.

It didn't matter.

The Janissary moved toward the window. It was large and thick with grime. The room overlooked a subway station, but now that place was covered with blood and bodies.

The Janissary smacked his hand into the glass, sending shards to rain down on the ground. He crawled into the window frame and jumped out.

He landed in a sprawl on the ground.

A group of cronux were on the tracks. Not mindless killers like the others. These bugs had evolved for purpose. They were small creatures with no mouths, and they would serve until they had no strength left, then they would curl up and die. For now, they moved like large spiders with massive fingers, building and tweaking components.

An upright green pool flashed with electricity as the bugs worked.

Others were entering in through the doorway, carrying components they had scavenged. The Janissary watched them with his newly grown eyes, and turned to look at the construction they were carrying out.

Another flash of green electricity and a mad claw reached through from the other side. It grabbed one of the bugs and smashed it in its grip for no apparent reason, just the madness of it all.

The light cut and the arm was severed. It fell to the ground and flopped around like a dying fish.

The Janissary looked down at it, considering for the moment the dull nature of his brothers.

It didn't matter.

Soon things would be finished.

And his mission would be complete.

18

WHEN ALICE WINTERS went through university, she had a military theorist class. The professor was clearly a lunatic. She could tell that by the way he wore his disheveled hair, or how he would pop the cap on his markers and smell the end of it before he drew on the board.

His classes were always her favorite.

"Right here," the professor had said as he drew a circle near the center of China. He tapped it and turned back to the class. "Lahnzu in the province of Gansu."

The professor, a shorter man with a rough beard, always rubbed the bristles on his chin when he was thinking. "That's where the spear would go. Right in the heart."

Alice remembered being so enthralled that she gave up scribbling notes and had instead turned on a recorder. She sat and listened to the man as he turned back to the board.

"A long time ago, some dumb asshole thought it was a good idea to start a city in-between two massive mountain ranges." He sat his blue pen down and picked up the red one. He popped the cap and sniffed the end of it. "Now that may not have been a problem for most of its lifespan, but after the Soviets got their Iron Curtain up to jam signals, there were problems. The Iron Curtain cast off electrical discharges."

He drew a swirl on the board, and then a line down toward the city. "Those discharges became Ion Storms that funnel down through those mountain valleys. They fried systems and made the whole damn place pretty uninhabitable during the storm season. But you don't have a society that's thousands of years old like the Chinese if you're a crybaby over a little killer storm here and there. So the Chinese spent billions of dollars hardening their systems, and they built this."

The professor walked over to his computer and typed a few buttons. The map went away on the board and a picture of a building, laying over the professor's scribbling, popped up on the screen.

He whistled and gestured. It was a picture from the ground looking up at a skyscraper that seemed to stretch on and on and on.

"This is the, uhh." He glanced back at the screen before shaking his head. "Oh hell, I never can say it right. Let's just call it the Lahnzu communications center. It's ninety-seven floors tall and fitted with a communications needle that extends messaging and signals beyond interference from even the Ion Storms, making it the most powerful communications center in all of China, rivaling even Beijing's own facilities to the point where the government decided to make it the focal point of communications for the country as a whole. This one building connects with all of China's communications, which may not sound all that impressive to an American, but is critical for the censor-obsessed Chinese and their moderators. The building has military security and defensive systems but you can bet . . ." He pressed some keys, bringing the map back up and walked over to the board. He picked up his blue marker again and popped the cap to sniff the end. He tapped a few blue dots on the center. ". . . this would be a key military objective in any war with China."

Alice remembered that all, but it came in a strange way. Like she had to walk over and pull it from the pile of memories. Just someone else's experiences being reported to her.

Some things were clear. Others were not.

It was hard to think these days.

And now, sitting in the back of a large eight wheel troop carrier, with a tangle of wet hair hung in front of her face, she worked that memory over like a sharp rock in her hand, the edges poking hard enough to draw blood.

It hurt.

It didn't all come either. Just bits and pieces. A fragmented reflection of her life, like a shattered mirror staring back at her.

It was hard to think. Easier to react.

Even now, in the back of the troop carrier, she could feel a dark presence looming over her.

The Archon.

It was as if he were right at her back, and his hand rested on her shoulder.

Waiting.

Watching.

He gave her the war.

"Go and take them," he'd said, his words becoming more and more human by the day.

She'd looked up at him, her eyes streaked with tears for reasons she didn't understand.

She didn't say anything. She didn't have to.

He knew her inside and out.

There was no resistance.

Only obedience.

And somehow, in a dark and twisted way, she loved him for it.

Love? Was that the right word?

It couldn't be, could it?

If it was, then why did it hurt so much?

Why would love want to rip your soul out?

Why would love make you do such ugly things?

Alice felt the rattle of the truck, and something shifted at her feet.

She wasn't alone.

The Archon might not be here in body, but others were.

A large beast with a snaking head and a mouth with three sets of jaws lay at her feet like a loyal dog. Infected once-men sat in their seats, their dull faces staring at the ground in front of them.

A long-limbed nightmare clung to the ceiling, and each bounce on the road made its body bob up and down.

Alice looked over at them and felt a tear streak down her face.

She started to sob like a child, her head rattling on her neck, a dark sense of confusion and fear rolling over her.

Why?

What was there to cry about?

This was a *gift*.

The Archon, her god, had given her a *gift*.

He trusted her.

What greater reward was there than to be chosen? To be worthy of a god's trust?

Alice's hands went up into her hair and she pulled and screamed.

The creatures stirred, but it was only with mild concern.

"This would be a key military objective in any war with China."

That was the professor again, and that thought flooded over all others.

She could see him. Marker in hand. Cap off.

Sniffing.

Was she there now?

He tapped his pen on the board.

Tick-tick-tick.

He sniffed the edge.

He capped it.

"That's where the spear would go. Right in the heart," he said again, starting the whole thing over.

The building.

The storm.

The war.

There were flashes of something else. Like a voice off in the distance calling out as it drowned.

Get out.

Get out.

Get out.

But where was there to go? What else was there to do but to serve the one she loved?

What greater honor could there be but to carry his war?

What more was there than to bend at the knee and await his command?

The Archon had grasped her chin and tilted her head. He understood her in ways no one else did.

She was valuable to him. She understood people in ways he did not.

She could fight the war in ways he couldn't understand.

She loved him.

He loved her.

She was worthy.

What more could there possibly be than to be valuable to a *god*?

"That's where the spear would go. Right in the heart," the professor said, the marker in hand.

He tapped the pen. She could hear it.

Tick-tick-tick.

And the blood, she could taste.

Off in the distance, in the garrisons along the border of China, the horde was fighting.

Alice had left them there.

They could draw attention.

Make it easy for one truck to move unseen.

"Some dumb asshole," the professor said and popped the cap on one pen.

Alice started crying again.

Why?

She didn't know why.

Tears ran down her face and she sobbed.

The flesh on her new arm, the one the Archon had grown for her, bubbled and writhed.

She wanted to tear it off.

But she didn't.

Why did she want to tear it off? Why did she not do it?

It was hard to think.

Easier to react.

"Some dumb asshole."

Sniff.

Tick-tick-tick.

The truck stopped with a jolt.

Alice snapped up her helmet from the seat alongside her and sat it on her head. Her head rolled back as the helmet sank down and the screens connected.

They were at the building.

She could see it.

From the eyes of the birds flying above.

For in this world, she had many eyes.

Now, when she spoke, she did not shout.

Only whispered.

"Now."

The four-legged beast at her feet came to life with a roar.

Two once-men at the back of the truck pulled the handles and stepped out, flooding the interior with daylight.

The four-legged creature bounded out, and the world filled with screams.

Alice took up her rifle and jumped out the back, her CAG boots connecting with the asphalt.

The massive communications building loomed just before her. The people walking in front of the building screamed and ran, while automated cars roared by Alice's parked truck.

She aimed the rifle and fired.

Her body here, but her mind elsewhere.

People ran.

People screamed.

Some fell.

She felt nothing.

The once-men poured out of the truck with her, grabbing victims as they ran, and Alice felt the parasites wiggling into their brains and taking over. Her mind stretched ever further.

She looked up. It was a bright and sunny day.

Untypical for the season.

Large towering skyscrapers reached up toward the sky.

The four-legged beast jumped into the road and knocked a car aside and into another, making both crash while others swerved past them.

Sound indicators on her CAG screen flashed as they reduced the volume.

A car flipped over and the beast plowed its head into the underbelly. It bit down and ripped pieces out and shoved the car into the metal median. More cars raced up but came to a jolting stop as the automation avoided damage. The beast turned on them and leapt onto the first, shoved its head down through the glass and ripped someone out. It only chewed twice before moving on.

Alice pulled her focus from it as she moved toward the entrance of the communications building. Once-men rushed past her, their numbers growing with each scream. Security guards with panicked eyes bolted the glass doors shut and backed away.

The infected slammed against it, and their wet hands streaked across the glass.

Move.

Alice ordered through the hive mind.

They parted in the center and she tucked her head down low as she rushed.

A few feet from the entrance and she hurled herself into the glass.

The strength of the CAG sent her bursting through and threw shards everywhere. Creatures came pouring through the gap instantly.

Security men with pistols took cover behind desks and scanners to fire their weapons. Several shots dinged off Alice's armor with flashes of red.

She tucked the rifle butt into her shoulder and aimed at one man.

Her shots blew into his stomach as bullet casings ejected from the barrel. Creatures rushed past her and clambered over gates. Alice moved steadily forward, her rifle up. A guard came from behind a scanner with a shotgun. He fired a round that blasted into Alice's head; her CAG flashed deep red. The force of it knocked her over.

She looked to see a once-man leaping the scanner and the two tumbled out of view.

A security guard aiming from behind a desk with a rifle fired into the once-men; red flashes of blood burst into the air with each of his shots. Alice came to her feet and aimed. She moved forward, head down, and fired two rounds, making red pops on the man's chest.

Another man screamed at her in Chinese and fired. Rounds clicked off Alice's CAG and her screen flashed red. She turned to see him duck behind a counter.

A howling once-man, with an insectile claw sprouting from his back, sprung over the desk.

Alice turned away as the man screamed.

More people came and Alice started to shift away, but only in mind.

Her body was still here. Moving on instinct alone, firing the rifle as men took positions.

But how could they hold back the flood?

She was the Archon's warrior.

He had given her this war.

Alice rushed through a metal detector and it screamed warnings and flashed red and yellow lights.

"That's where the spear would go. Right in the heart," the professor said, the marker in hand.

The rifle kicked in her arm.

A man's head split down the middle in a red burst.

Down the hallway, a small group of CAG-armored soldiers came out of a room; one held a shield while others fired around him. They moved like a block toward Alice.

A rifle shot impacted her, and her arm was knocked backward. An intense red flash came on her screen.

More shots burst around her, breaking down the walls.

A fat infected man leapt in front of her and absorbed the hits with his body while Alice ducked into a crevice.

She pressed the release on the rifle magazine, letting it clatter to the ground, and slammed a fresh mag in.

Infected went screaming past her position, and then fire burst into the hallway, cooking them as they charged.

She stuck her head around the corner and saw the CAG soldiers still tight behind the shield, and firing rifles and a flame thrower.

New thoughts flooded into Alice's head. They were from the dead security guards.

Their minds connected with the hive mind, and now she knew what they knew.

Alice came away from the wall and looked toward a secure metal door.

More infected went screaming past her as she ran to the door. She threw her leg into it and kicked hard into the center, making it dent.

Alice kicked it hard again with her heel and it broke inward with a groan. She leaned back and threw her shoulder into it.

The door cracked inward under the CAG's strength and Alice spilled into the room.

There was a wide-eyed man hiding in the corner. He said nothing as Alice went past him, but the infected came behind her and filled the room with screams. Alice ran toward a room on the opposite side and lowered her shoulder. It was a simple wooden door and she burst through it. She lost her footing and smacked into the plaster wall on the other side and left a spider-web hole in the wall.

She came to her feet and moved to the hallway, coming back to the center.

She was behind the CAG soldiers now.

One was in the center, holding a shield with his rifle propped up and firing. Another was on his left, his rifle up and his elbows tucked low for positioning. The third had a flamethrower that burst and filled the hallway.

Alice charged them from behind, and the flame soldier glanced over his shoulder with just enough time to see her land a solid kick into his back.

The man went skidding face-first on the ground. Infected leapt on top of him and pried the weapon away.

The soldier with the shield twisted around and Alice slammed her fist into his helmet, hard enough to knock him over. The rifle soldier bowled into Alice and knocked her backward. Alice smashed into a wall and the man aimed his rifle and fired.

Rounds impacted her waist and Alice twisted with her arm up.

A bullet went through her arm guard and black blood splashed up on the wall.

It was her new arm.

She moved to come off the wall, but the soldier fired again and a round impacted her chest, knocking her back again.

Infected slammed into the man and knocked him to the ground. His rifle kept firing but Alice turned away and looked down the hall to the elevators.

An unarmored security guard in front of the elevator doors beat his hands against the buttons. He stared at Alice, his eyes wide, as she closed in, black blood dripping from her arm.

She lowered her rifle, but continued forward.

Her armor flashed yellow warnings over and over indicating the compromise in her arm guard.

She reached up to the clasps above her elbow and cracked them open, and slid the armored sleeve off.

It fell to the ground and her horrible arm cracked and extended now that it was free of the tight armor.

Some poor soul that had been hiding safely made a desperate run past Alice, but a one-armed infected man thrust his insectile appendage through the man's chest, making blood spray and hit the white walls by the elevator. Speckles of red began to drip down almost immediately.

The frantic man at the elevator dropped his jaw and slammed his hand into the button again.

All he was doing was calling and canceling the elevator over and over again, making the call button light up, and darken with each hit.

It didn't matter. It wouldn't speed the elevator up.

The numbers above the door read:

Sixty-seven.

Sixty-six.

Sixty-five.

The man smashed the button again.

A once-man came screaming past Alice, half of its face gone, and it dove into the man. It hit hard enough that they both smashed into the wall and toppled over.

The man struggled and wrestled with it as Alice took his place in front of the elevator.

But she was far more patient.

She pressed the button only once.

19

JOHN HAD both hands out as he leaned down to a table. It was covered in documents.

The gray-haired White House lawyer, the same man who had served John while in the Senate, sat in a chair. His jacket was off and his sleeves rolled up. His thin-framed glasses sat on the table.

"They're enacting the McCarthy clause, Mr. President." The lawyer rubbed his temples. "The bastards really want you."

John looked over the documents. Some of them were pictures of American aircraft flying over Berlin.

"What does this all mean?" John said, but he already knew.

The lawyer put his hand down and gave John a flat look. "Means they're going to brand you a traitor. The moment you cleared those jets to enter Soviet territory in defense of the Soviets in Berlin, you made yourself a mark. The McCarthy clause forbids a sitting president to authorize any military action that would directly benefit the Soviets for any reason without congressional approval. The Senate is selecting their counselors right now and they'll decide if you should be removed."

"Who appoints the counselors?" John asked, still looking away from the pictures to read a document laid out in front of him.

"If you keep asking me questions you already know the answer to, we're going to be here all night. It hasn't changed since you were in the Senate. It's the majority leader. Tom McIntyre."

John shot him a look. "Cut me a little slack. I'm planning a war, arguing foreign trade agreements, and I feel like I've only slept for about twenty minutes in the last two weeks."

"Yeah, yeah," the lawyer nodded his head and spoke with a more forgiving tone. He leaned forward and put his glasses back on. "Here's what's going to happen. They'll form the council within the next few days at the latest, tomorrow at the earliest. There will be a closed door deliberation, and then the preliminary findings will be announced. If the council concludes that there's valid evidence, they'll trigger the McCarthy clause and there will be a stay of leadership while an investigation is conducted. The Sergeant at Arms will be sent here to remove you for the duration of the proceedings. The vice president will assume office, but given that there is none, it will fall to the Speaker of the House."

"Hayward," John said with a nod of his head. He leaned off the table. "You know she proposed a bill to cut all support from the Soviets and bring our forces back here?"

"She's stewing up the base for the next election cycle. Dead communist always drive the numbers." The lawyer huffed and shook his head. "But is it a bad idea to cover our own asses before we worry about anyone else's?"

John stopped and glared at him. "You think those things in New York care who is American and who isn't? If the Soviets fold, then those forces will consolidate in Europe and when they're all dead where do you think they're going to go? We'll outlive the Europeans, but it'll be the Australians or the Chinese who are the last to go. That's the same game plan as McIntyre and the others. Pull back and defend our own, let the aliens finish off our enemies, and pray we can do better than the Soviets."

The lawyer held his hand up. "I get it. I'm no military strategist."

John shook his head. "It's not even just military. There's a bill being whipped in the Senate right now that'll restrict the trade of weapons and medical supplies from the States, but I just spent the last twelve hours negotiating with the Sudanese to bolster the defenses of the Egyptians as the horde out of Iran starts to pour in. They only agreed if we supplied the weapons. There are already outbreaks, but if the horde breaks into Africa, it won't just be the millions of civilians that'll get swallowed up and turned into enemy soldiers, it also means the mineral trade will collapse. We'll be totally reliant on Venezuela's lithium and cobalt to keep up with munitions and CAG replacements, and with the peace accords shattered, those have grown to a halt."

The lawyer shook his head. "It's all above my pay grade."

John shook his head and grabbed a bottle of water. He twisted off the cap to take a drink. "Sorry, I just feel like I need to strangle someone these days."

"I can't help you with that either, but here's what I can suggest." He tapped his finger on a document. "You want to fight the McCarthy clause? The language is murky, but if I'm being honest here, you're playing a losing hand. You'd do better to call up McIntyre and see if you can still cut a deal for him to back off. If you throw him a bone to chew on, he might leave you alone."

John shook his head. "You don't know the man like I do. All he sees is spin, but I'll give him the call regardless."

The lawyer leaned back in the chair and rubbed his chin. "You told me not to tell you what they say on the news."

"Yeah, I know how Washington does business and I don't want any of it to get under my skin. I don't need to hear any of it."

The lawyer closed his eyes and shook his head. "You'll need to hear this before you talk to McIntyre."

John twisted his head. "All right, what is it then?"

"They're saying you pulled strings to get Alice out of Libya before Tripoli fell."

John took a deep breath. "It's true. I did. I'll say as much."

"They're going to say you're putting everyone else's sons and daughters all around the world for politics when you wouldn't do it with your own."

"I know what they'll say."

"That's not the half of it either. It's about your wife."

"What the hell do they have to say about Cora?"

"Not her, they're talking about Gina. There are rumors going around that you were sleeping with Cora while Gina was getting the treatments. That shit head on Lift News brought it up in an interview with McIntyre. They had some doctors on to talk about Eli too."

John squeezed one hand tight but held the other flat to the lawyer. "I don't need to hear anymore of it. I can't stop them from talking, so all it can do is get under my skin. Between you and me though, I wasn't seeing anyone while Gina was getting treatments."

The lawyer frowned. "You didn't have to tell me that, I know who you are. Some will believe it though. Everyone in Washington has a boyfriend or a girlfriend."

John stiffened his face and shook his head. "Not me."

"Yeah. Why do you think they hate you so much?"

JOHN LEFT the meeting and moved through the halls of the White House. As a senator, he'd been here before, but the place was always brimming with life.

Now large portions of the staff were gone, and anyone that required Senate approval was stuck in limbo.

He'd spent the last few days balancing diplomacy, economics, and coordinating the counterattack of New York City.

Through all of that, it was sometimes easy to miss all the bad press.

"McIntyre was on the news again," his secretary told him as she joined him in the hallway.

John held up a hand. "I've heard. And if it's anything new, I don't have the brain power to deal with it right now. Let him sling his mud if he wants, I don't have time to dwell on it."

With a tight, sympathetic smile, she nodded her head. "I'll prepare your afternoon schedule."

"Thank you."

John approached the dining room and saw Cora waiting outside with Eli, her hand on his shoulder. She wore a sad but bright smile; Eli even grinned as John approached.

John held his arms out wide. "Sweetie, come here." He moved close and grabbed her tight for a hug. He then reached down and wrapped his arm around Eli bringing him up. "God it's good to see you two."

Cora patted his back. "I was wondering when you'd be able to carve out a minute for us."

"You'd know what I'd give to have dinner with you two and sleep in my own bed at night?"

"I get it, I get it." She grinned but it didn't touch her eyes. "The country needs you more than we do."

John smiled back and then looked up at the door. "Why are you two waiting out here? No one let you in?"

"We didn't see anybody," Eli said, and tugged at his shirt collar.

John huffed and shook his head. "We're on a skeleton staff here, Cora. The damn Senate is slow-walking all of my appointees and I don't even have a chief of staff." He opened the door and let her in. "Thank God we still have a cook though."

Cora grinned and kissed him on the cheek. John patted Eli's shoulder and guided him toward a chair. "What do you want to eat buddy? Hamburger? Maybe pizza?"

"I'm not hungry," Eli moaned as he took a seat. He pulled an action figure out of his pocket and started to pose it on the table.

"Eli, sweetie. You *have* to eat," Cora said in a strong tone.

"I don't want to." He kept bending the toy and sitting it up.

"John, he hasn't been eating. It's been a fight every day to get him to eat or go to sleep."

John frowned. "He's been through a lot, Cora."

"John, he *doesn't eat*. I don't mean he only wants chips, I mean he won't eat anything at all."

John patted his hand on Eli's back. "Buddy, you have to eat if you want to keep growing. You have to eat *something*."

Eli's head rolled up in a slow movement and his gaze settled on John. "I'm not hungry. I'm never hungry."

John felt a chill creep up his spine. He took a seat next to Eli and stroked his back for a few moments. "Tell you what, buddy, if you eat a hamburger today, we'll all have a little ice cream after, how's that sound?"

Eli grinned. "Okay."

John flashed a look to Cora, but the attendant entered. They each gave him an order and when he left, John forced on a grin. "So how has studying been going?"

"We finished," Eli said.

"Finished?" He glanced toward Cora.

"All the books. He's completed all the workbooks up until third grade. I ordered the next three grades and they should be here tomorrow." Cora smiled, but again, it didn't touch her eyes. "He's a very smart boy, John, very impressive."

"That's great, buddy, I love to hear that you're studying hard."

"It's all easy." He bent the toy and posed it on the table again.

Cora laughed under her breath. "Most of the other kids his age are still barely reading single words, but he's flying through textbooks and doing higher level math. He can already name every country in the Americas on a map."

John took a sharp breath. "Hey, he's a genius, just like his mother."

"Did mommy read a lot of books too?"

"Maybe not as many as you, but she liked to read."

Cora frowned "John, your eyes are red. When was the last time you slept?"

"I sleep a few hours every night, don't worry about me. There's just a lot of work to do now until I get a new chief of staff."

"That's dangerous, John. Both for you and the country."

"You're not telling me anything I don't know, but I can't trust half the people in Washington. They call it a wolf pit for a reason. Cora, you're the only person I'd consider putting in the job right now if I thought for a moment you'd take it."

"I wouldn't know the first thing about politics."

"You don't give yourself enough credit, I think you'd jump right in."

"How about me?" Eli asked.

"You? You look like ambassador material to me. How about being ambassador to France, Eli?" John grinned.

"No," Eli said flatly, staring at his action figure. "That wouldn't be fun."

"Why not?" John asked. "They've got great food and you could take a look at the Eiffel Tower."

His gaze flicked up. "But all those people are dying. I don't think it would be fun."

John felt his stomach sink. He looked up at Cora. "Are you telling him about everything?"

She shook her head. "Believe me, I don't tell him a word and I don't turn on the TV. I certainly don't want to see any of those interviews. The things they are saying about us are horrible. " She gave a knowing look to John.

John ground his teeth but looked away. "These people, Cora . . . they burn the whole thing down if they think they can get a bigger bite. Don't let them get under your skin."

"Get under *my* skin?" Her eyes widened. "I'm not the one with the anger problem, Mr. President."

"I don't have the energy for anger these days. I cook enough brain cells to get the job done and that's about it." John forced a smile. "Let's talk about something else for the next thirty minutes. I've had enough with work."

The attendant came in with the hamburgers and set them all out.

"Remember the deal," John pointed at Eli with mock seriousness. "First the burger and then the ice cream."

Eli nodded wildly and dug into the burger.

John reached over and patted Cora's arm.

They shared a smile, and he rubbed her arm but said nothing.

It was nice to have a moment to do nothing but eat with the people he loved.

The door opened up and John's secretary came in. "Mr. President,

Mr.—" Roles followed behind her. "I tried to stop him, sir, but he insisted."

"Mr. President, we need to talk," Roles said.

"Can it wait, Roles? I'm only asking for thirty minutes."

Roles looked at both Cora and Eli and nodded his head. "I'll be waiting out here." He pulled the door closed himself.

"I swear, if he interrupted to tell me about what McIntyre's saying on TV I'm going to have every TV in the White House thrown out."

John got his thirty minutes, and he tried to flush everything out of his mind and focus only on Cora and Eli. He tried to bring up cartoons, but Eli ended up retelling everything he'd learned in their history while Cora and John ate.

John noticed that Eli was only picking at his food, so John looked at his attendant. "They have chocolate syrup for the ice cream back there, right?"

"Yes sir, and sprinkles," the attendant said with a nod.

That was enough prompting for Eli to finish the rest of the food.

Cora flashed a smile to him, and it wasn't five minutes later that they were bringing out the ice cream. Eli was deadly focused on it, while John put his hand on Cora's.

"How are you?" he asked.

"Never better, just wish I could see you a bit more. How about you spend the night with us? I think one of the privileges of being president is that no one will tell you that you can't sleep in your own bed."

John grinned but shook his phone. "I need to connect with the Japanese and Australian trade negotiations tonight."

"Don't you have a minister in place for it?"

"I do, but the two sides need a kick in the rear to come to terms, and they're both far more polite if I'm listening."

There was a loud clunk as Eli dropped his spoon on his empty plate, having finished the ice cream.

Cora leaned in and whispered, *"You're truly a statesman,"* as Eli licked the ice cream glass.

"Just have to find the right buttons to push is all." He grinned and patted her on the back. "I have to get back to work now, or Roles is going to charge in here and strangle me."

"I really am worried about you not having the help you need, John. You need someone to run the schedule at least."

"Recruitment is a top priority, honey. There's a war in New York, but I still have a hundred calls a day about trade and the economy. A lot of these morons in congress don't understand that it's not just about where you place the troops, but what they have to eat, and how fast you can make their bullets, and none of that works if the people back home can't buy bread at the store."

John escorted the two out, and true to his word, Roles was sitting on a nearby bench. He rose and put his hands behind his back, and nodded to both Cora and Eli as they passed. "Mrs. Winters."

John watched them leave before turning back to Roles.

"Couldn't make a call?" John asked.

Roles shook his head. "Some things need to be said in person."

"All right then." John motioned toward the Oval Office and they started down the hallway. "Can you believe those bastards in Congress won't give us a full staff despite everything that's going on?"

"They want to bleed you out and put their own person in charge."

John opened the door and let Roles enter.

"And what do you think?" John asked as he closed the door and moved to his desk. "I'm starting to think it'd be better for the country if I stepped aside and let them have it."

Roles stood stiff backed and emotionless. "Mr. President, frankly, you're the only one I trust to hold the wheel."

"That makes one of us, but I'll be damned if I let McIntyre get his slimy hands on the presidency. God only knows what that bastard would do to us. I'm sure he would let what's left of the Soviet Union scatter to the wind and cut the heels of the Chinese if he could. Until these bastards understand this is all bigger than any one of us, we're going to have to hold things down. But if I don't get help to manage the schedule again, I might just have a heart attack and make the whole issue moot. But what is it you needed to tell me?"

"John," Roles said in the most empathetic tone John had ever heard from him. "It's Alice. She sent the Chinese a message."

"What?" John scoffed. "She's alive?"

"No, John." Roles pressed a button on his datapad and handed it to John. It was an image of Alice's face with purple veins.

"She's one of them."

20

A DEAD BODY slumped against a wall like a cast-off toy, and dried blood streaked down the white paint.

Moller was beside it, sitting on her ass with her legs out.

A deep hiss from the throat of a cronux filled the air.

Moller stayed still. With no weapon, and too heavy to run, playing dead was all she had.

A massive creature like a tadpole with long, thin arms crawled into the room. It dragged a thick, squirming tail across broken glass, careless of the speckles of black blood it left in its trail.

It had no head, just a set of massive jaws set within its gut, and its massive mouth opened wide, stringing spit. It croaked as its heavy body slithered fully into the room.

It was hunting her.

She was cautious, but the deeper she got into the city, the more there were.

She moved on the streets only when she had to, and when she could, she would get into a building and cross through it.

There were fewer in the buildings, but there were still some.

Like this ugly shithead.

Moller kept her head still, but her eyes followed it. She was close enough that she could touch, and that strange suicidal part of the brain asked her, *why not?*

But her hand was still, and she played possum.

The hellspawn tadpole moved through her room, and its massive tail swung over her leg as it turned, hunting her presence.

The dull beast wouldn't find her. The armor worked. So long as she didn't move or make any noise, it wouldn't know she was here.

The armor had been reinforced to hide even her heartbeat. The creature twisted and turned its large head, the whole thing bending in a way only possible with flexible bones.

It had three long fingers and it palmed the ground to drag its heavy body forward while the tail shifted like a snake.

It had blood on its face. It had killed recently.

But as she watched it, the long fingers straining for a hold so as to drag forward, she had to wonder, *why the hell does such a thing exist?*

Was there a purpose for being so hideous? Did it convey some advantage?

Or was that the point of it? To be so horrible and painful for itself as it was for others?

God, she hated the damn things.

The tadpole aimed its large jaws at her for a moment.

A long moment.

And though Moller knew it couldn't hear her, she held her breath.

The spit slid down its teeth, and a fat glob of snot slapped onto the floor.

With a disappointed bellow, it turned away and crawled from the room.

Moller waited two minutes for it to pass before she rolled over to her knees and climbed up to her feet. The armor was a bitch to move in, and twice as bad to stand up from, but she learned quickly it was best to just drop to her ass. She lost count of how many times she had to play possum, but the first time one came near her, she froze in place. She had to stand on her feet, unmoving for a solid twenty minutes, which didn't sound like much until you had to do it a few times in the span of just a couple hours.

She'd already been in the city for a day, and despite the stims to keep her awake, she was still exhausted.

It didn't matter.

She had inched her way into the center past stalking beasts and a flowing horde.

It was easier to move when the horde was nearby. It made enough noise that she could head through a building and they'd drown out her presence.

That still didn't mean she wanted to be anywhere near it though.

And that's what the horde was—an *it*. A near-singular mass of crawling limbs and pointed claws. It moved so tightly, she couldn't imagine how anything inside it was able to move at all.

It was a rolling pile of flesh that devoured everything in its wake.

Moller did her best to stay the hell away from it. When it was possible, she'd get into a building and move to the second floor.

It made for slow travel, but slow was better than dead, and the ceilings and walls of a building helped make sure there wasn't something crawling just out of sight.

She looked around the room she was in now. It was dark inside, but her helmet picked up the ambient light.

It was time to get moving, but she decided for a systems check.

She tapped a few keys on her wrist guard and a power gauge popped up and flashed yellow—time for a recharge.

She looked around the broken office building. It was scattered with paper, broken furniture, and shards of glass. A single computer monitor was knocked over, but still functioning silently. The screen had a video streaming service ending one show and counting down to begin another.

She blinked hard and wanted to scratch the itch on her forehead, but there was no way in hell that was going to happen. Instead, she bent over and picked up a piece of a broken chair. She hurled it at the wall on the opposite side. It cracked into the white drywall and clattered to the ground.

Moller froze in place and listened.

Nothing.

She was safe.

Content, she cracked open the hatch on her elbow guard and twisted out the spent filter block. It steamed and she dropped it onto the floor as she dug out another and pounded it in.

Her gauge flashed twice and then went green.

She looked over to a window and decided she better go have a look and see where she was at.

But at the same time, it was hard to move.

She was so tired.

Her eyes felt heavy, and she was sure if she blinked too long she might pass out.

It was time to juice again.

The armor had an internal stim system. She just punched it into her wrist controls and a second later she felt the prick in the back of her neck.

Getting the injection into the meat of her neck had sickened her before. She'd always loaded it up in the arm like everyone else, but research was saying that the neck was the best place. It helped the distribution spread more evenly or something or other. Wasn't her field of expertise for certain.

The stim came in like ice water and made her shudder. She'd heard others describe it like a jolt, or even a burning. Why it felt like ice water to her and hot to another was a mystery for the ages.

She closed her eyes and shivered as it spread.

Just as good as a cup of iced coffee, except it was more like eight cups and it was injected directly into the bloodstream.

Moller went to the window and looked out just fast enough to see the damn tadpole slither down the stairs of a subway entrance. Moller put her hand up onto the window rest and watched carefully.

Other creatures went in and out, but there were also infected people carrying things down. A naked fat man with a massive stomach wound dragged his guts and a large fuel cell the size of a bathtub for God knows what reason. The man stepped on a strand of his intestines and tripped. He dashed his face into a parking curb. With no real concern at all, he got back up to his feet, teeth falling out of his mouth, and grabbed onto the cell again. A large beast, the same shape and size as a tiger, came up out of the subway entrance and batted the man aside. The man smacked into the ground and rolled a few feet away as the tiger-like monster bit into a corner of the cell and dragged it down the stairs.

"The hell is going on . . ." Moller said under her breath. She'd never seen them act that way.

The fat man climbed back up to his feet again and headed back toward where he'd come from.

Moller reached up for the dial on her helmet and rotated it, zooming in. She saw one infected carrying an armful of laptops. Another had what looked like an exhaust pipe. A small group dragged a massive antenna.

All headed toward the subway tunnel.

She had to get inside, but there were too many heading in and out.

How the hell was she supposed to get in with so many like that?

Moller watched for a few minutes.

The stims were still juicing in her system, but she was still tired. It was all mental. A combination of a long, irritating itch, and the necessity of having to piss in the armor seal for a few hours.

But she was in too deep to quit now.

She pulled a fuel cell out of an elbow sheath then loaded it in right next to the filter. It made a strange *pop* sound as the injector pierced it when she locked the unit in place.

She didn't feel any different but she would soon shed a boosted amount of radiation. She sat still and waited for the fuel cells to take full effect while the group of infected dragged the antenna closer.

She climbed up into the window and watched the group dragging the antenna, and there were dozens coming and going from the subway.

Too crowded to breach.

Sometimes all there was left to do was roll the dice.

Moller leapt from the window, the powerful armor adding strength and throwing her forward. She hurtled through the air, and her helmet screen painted a yellow line of her trajectory directly into the crowd dragging the antenna.

She smashed into them, and hit with enough power that she crushed every bone in at least two of them.

The creatures frenzied and shrieked with their tentacles flailing.

Moller rolled across the ground and hugged the antenna.

Only two of the infected could still move, the others were little more than sacks of flesh writhing on the ground. They attacked her, screaming as their tentacles slithered over her.

But Moller didn't move. She didn't react.

She only held onto the antenna.

The massive arm of the tadpole came from nowhere to smack them away. Moller was close enough now that when it opened its jaws, she stared down into its gut, and at the rows of teeth lining its throat.

It bit down onto the end of the antenna and dragged.

Moller's armor scratched across the concrete, leaving a long white mark.

The tadpole backed down the stairs and Moller held tighter. They thumped down, and each step felt like it rattled her brain.

Moller kept her head in place, but she saw that the deeper they went in, the more there were.

The infected pressed themselves to the wall, and dark purple slime crawled out of their mouths and wounds, covering everything. They were using their bodies to coat the damn walls.

Moller felt her blood run cold. They were changing the environment.

The tadpole dragged her onto the dark purple fleshy ground like she had seen in Russia. A crawling skin that was inching further and further.

All at once, Moller wished she could let go and run out. Everything inside her told her to get up and run before she went any deeper.

Instead, she just held on.

She couldn't feel it, but she could see the purple flesh rub up her side as she was dragged in, like fingers wiping against her. It would stretch up and rub over her helmet and the sensors on her screen indicated contact.

She was dragged into a thicker crowd and passed through the legs of walking infected. There were so many that the tadpole dropped the antenna and roared to make the crowd part.

The antenna dragged closer, and Moller looked around without moving her head. She spotted an infected soldier. He still had his helmet on, but one arm was gone and a long tentacle hung from it. She passed him, her eyes tracing him, but the man's head swiveled to watch her.

The infected started walking along beside her, his chin pointed down to her as if he were looking.

Moller held her breath.

He bumped into another creature and the two fell over, and Moller was dragged into the subway station. The hallway opened up into the wide main platform, and strangely, the crowds were thinner here. Moller slowly bent her head. She could see they were building something massive on the rails. It was a strange half-built circle, and there were small insectile creatures crawling around it, threading wire and snapping pieces into place. The purple skin grew all around it, and spilled out the base.

The tadpole dropped the antenna with a thud and climbed down over the edge. It bit into it again and pulled. It dragged the antenna to the side until it all fell. It shifted as it slid off and Moller ended up underneath. The antenna smacked into her and her screen flashed yellow, indicating an attack.

She let her arms loose and the antenna dragged away while she hugged up against the side of the wall at the base of the platform.

The construction came alive with a burst of green and blue light. It popped and fizzed as an upright pool of green waved in and out.

A long, pale tentacle slithered out and felt around. It grabbed one of the insectile creatures working on the construction. The tentacle wrapped around the creature and squeezed it. There was a pop of air that almost sounded like a scream as the little insect's head exploded. The tentacle dropped it and slithered around for more.

The light cut and the tentacle was sliced off from the root.

It fell into the purple skin and flapped like a dying fish as the skin oozed around it and sucked it down.

They were making a gate.

Moller had to go tell someone. She shifted her head and looked around the room. She either had to climb back up and head up the stairs, or try to make her way down one of the tunnels.

She stopped.

A tall thing on two legs jumped down off the edge of the platform down to the rails and approached the construction.

The Janissary.

Though Moller had seen images of the Archon, she hadn't seen any of the Janissary, but she knew it instantly. It moved with a sense of purpose that the others didn't have.

Somehow the damn thing had gotten from Russia to here.

The Janissary walked over to the gate, but stopped and shifted its head toward her.

It had black glossy eyes.

They focused on her.

"Shit," Moller whispered.

The Janissary shifted up, its whole body extending taller as its tail waved behind it.

Moller froze in place without so much as breathing.

The Janissary tilted its head down like a prowling lion and it came forward.

Moller could hear the crack of rock beneath its feet as it closed in. The gate came to life again and went off behind it, flashing green light in the room.

The Janissary's two-toed foot stepped right by Moller's head. It reached down and grabbed her helmet, a fat thumb pressing up against one of the helmet cams with a loud squeak. It lifted her up from the ground with complete ease, gripping her head like a basketball.

Moller fought the urge to kick and run; instead she went loose and played dead again as it lifted her face right up to it.

169

She saw into its black eyes as the Janissary stared into her screen.

"Sol-*dier*." Its voice was a bubbling growl. It placed its other hand by her neck and squeezed. Instantly her helmet flashed and screen indicators popped up showing massive pressure.

It was going to tear her helmet off.

With a sudden burst of panic, Moller kicked and punched at it.

The Janissary dropped her, more from surprise than anything else. Moller fell down to her ass and crawled back. A light flashed, showing a compromise in her suit's neck guard.

The Janissary twisted its head and paced forward at her.

"Oh shit, oh shit." Moller scrambled back as the Janissary moved in quickly and grabbed her. It lifted her into the air, intent to rip her head off. "Get off me!" Moller said as she punched and kicked.

It wasn't concerned at all. It only slowly looked her over then grabbed her side again.

Moller screamed while her suit flashed.

Breach. Breach. Breach.

A biohazard sign flashed with it.

Moller reached down to her elbow sheath and pulled out the rest of the fuel cells, just as the Janissary wrapped its fingers around her head again. She stuck them up into its face and squeezed her hand into a fist.

They burst out with a puff of yellow smoke with silver flashes in it.

The Janissary scrambled back, screeching and batting at its eyes.

Moller held one hand to her neck where the armor broke and got to her feet. She rushed into the darkness of the subway tunnel as the Janissary screamed.

21

TWO HOURS AGO, Zhao had a call with the governess of Gansu. She had the unfortunate luck of relocating her estate to the city of Lahnzu just three months prior. Zhao had listened to her desperate pleas for troop reinforcements when the creatures broke in. Her terrified face had looked away and she screamed.

He pressed the *End Call* button on the screen and turned away.

He had no need nor desire to see the governess torn apart, and he had already seen Alice Winters' second video.

There would be no hiding that one. The news sources had fabricated ones that they would show and debunk as fake, in an attempt to cast doubt on the real one, but there were some things that could not be hidden.

Such as the death of the city of Lahnzu.

Zhao sat alone within his office, his hands clasped together as he stared at the wall, and considered ordering a series of strikes to destroy the city altogether, but no, at best that would be a temporary fix. There were other measures more important.

He needed to see the Dragon.

That was it then. He gathered his coat, made a few calls, and shortly after, he was there on the street, staring at the community center.

It had been a simple community complex once.

Now it was Beijing's own little slice of Hell on Earth.

The windows were blocked with blackened bodies that had pressed up and fused into place. The security officers, men and women in full CAG with open-face helmets, secured the perimeter now. They erected a large, mechanized fence around the area and focused spotlights onto the doors, windows, and roof. Hovercraft flew overhead, shining their lights around the area.

Wu approached him in a long coat, a lit cigarette in his mouth. Wu pulled the cigarette out of his mouth and bowed, if only for public appearances. "Chairman." When he leaned up, he looked to the security officer. "Show the Chairman what you showed me."

"*Sir,*" the officer said and snapped a quick bow. He pulled out a viewfinder and offered it to Zhao with both hands in a respectful gesture. "Sir, please look at the third window on the first floor of the east wing."

Zhao took it and zoomed in on the window. He was about to ask what it was he was supposed to see, and then he noticed.

A single white eye in the black mass. It moved around and looked. Never blinking. Always watching.

Zhao felt the hairs stand up on the back of his neck as he handed the viewfinder to the officer.

"Some are still alive?" he asked.

"Yes sir, it appears so, but the power has been cut and the perimeter secured. Nothing has come out."

"Except for the creature," Zhao said without pulling his eyes away from the building. "The one that requested my attendance."

"Yes sir. It fell over and died shortly after. We incinerated it to be certain."

Zhao nodded and unbuttoned his jacket. "Prepare an entryway. I will be going in."

The officer's eyes widened. "Sir, I will prepare an entry team to accompany you."

"No. It's impolite to bring uninvited guests." Zhao handed his jacket over.

The officer glanced down to the jacket with confusion, but held it politely with both hands. "Sir, a moment and I will gather armor."

Wu watched their exchange without speaking, the cigarette dangling from his mouth.

Zhao turned to look at the man with a cold stare. "If he intends to kill me, would the armor save my life? No, all I require is an electric torch and a rebreather as I suspect the smell of decay may be overwhelming. What we all do now, we do in service of the People's Republic." He pointed at his jacket. "Keep the jacket clean. It was a gift from my mother."

"Yes sir." The officer bowed his head deeply. When he looked up, he directed a junior officer, "Give him your rebreather!"

"Sir!" the junior officer shouted. He dug through his pack and bowed as he offered it with both hands to Zhao.

The senior officer snapped up straight again. "Sir, we do not have an electric torch. All of our lighting equipment is set within the helmets. All we have are light markers."

"Then give them to me."

The junior officer dug out a small plastic sleeve and bowed to offer them.

"Chairman," the senior officer said, "please allow me to fit you with audio equipment. If there is a disturbance, we will enter by force."

Wu exhaled. "If the Chairman needed your advice, he would request it. Do not position yourself to advise the Chairman on affairs you know little about. Know your place."

The officer snapped both hands down to his side and bowed once more. "Forgive me, sir."

Wu watched him for a moment and with the cigarette smoking between two fingers, he pointed at some recording equipment. "We'll need all recording equipment disabled for the time being, including armored recordings. It would not be good for morale to have the death of the Chairman recorded. Both of you, see it done."

Zhao flashed a hard look at Wu, but he did not disagree.

"Yes sir." The officer bowed his head to Wu and both he and the junior officer rushed off.

Zhao took a sharp breath. "You have a tongue."

"Bold and clear words are the only thing of value an advisor can offer his leader." Wu squinted his face and looked at the building. "I suspect you will not outlive the night."

"If I'm killed, see that the Dragon is not attacked. Send in a communications drone and see if further negotiations can be met. Then have all security personnel at this perimeter detained and replaced, and call a governor's assembly to install the next Chairman. The proper functions to show my death as a natural one are prepared and ready to be deployed. All other orders are in documentation form in the center drawer of my desk. I left it unlocked. If there's anything left of me, see that I am buried with that jacket. If there isn't, then bury the jacket in my place."

Wu held the cigarette between his teeth as he mumbled. "For the People's Republic."

"See it done," Zhao said. He turned around and rolled his sleeves up as he approached the gate entrance.

"Open the gate!" someone shouted, and the motorized gate came alive with a buzz and slid away.

Zhao fit the rebreather on his head and walked through. The security officers all bowed as he passed.

The rebreather gave a quiet whistle and a pop with each breath he took as he approached the building. Zhao pressed onto the community center door and it opened.

It was nearly pitch black inside except for small rays of light piercing through the coated windows, or the occasional spotlight from a hovercraft as it passed. But Zhao couldn't see far in. He took a small plastic sheet out of his pocket and twisted the top off and dropped it to the floor. He stripped out a white light marker. He snapped it and then shook it. A yellow-green light cast up.

The glow did not illuminate far, but he could better see the walls. There were strange, twisted bodies plastered as if they'd grown out of it. A thick purple mucus was radiating from each of them. Their barely recognizable faces were fixed in expressions of eternal torment.

There was a flicker of doubt as Zhao's hand twitched and he nearly dropped the glow stick and ran. But he was not one to give in to fear, and he was not a slave to fear.

He walked in.

The glow illuminated dust floating in the air—decay that made Zhao's eyes itch, but he fanned it away.

Shadows played on the corpses, making them appear to move.

Zhao went further in, past hallways, and to the entrance to the gymnasium.

The bodies were thicker now, and even the floor was lopsided with darkened, burned lumps. Zhao had to walk carefully lest he stumble.

And now that he was deeper in, he looked more closely and saw that it wasn't the shadows at all. The fingers and limbs on the wall did move and shift as if adjusting from discomfort.

He looked away and went to the center doors and pushed them wide. They opened to a large room with dried blood on the floor, and the same mucus on the wall. Tables, chairs, and medical equipment had been overturned and thrown around. A half-man stood fused to the ground not far away, but unlike the others, he was far more aware. His head shifted toward Zhao's direction.

A weaker man might have run, but Zhao was not a weaker man.

He entered. *"Dragon?"* he called out, and his voice was muffled from the rebreather. "You have called me and I have come. Where are you?" The glow stick began to die and Zhao dropped it to the floor. He slid out two more and cracked them. Holding one in his hand, he threw the other to the center of the room.

It lit up bodies of infected, crawling on the ground, their focus on Zhao.

Zhao took one step back and gasped, but he held his position. "Dragon?" he shouted even louder. "You have called and I have come. *Show yourself.*"

"Chairman," came a croak from further in.

175

Zhao straightened and went forward toward the crowd of infected. The man fused to the floor watched him pass and slowly lifted his hand toward Zhao. He could have grabbed him, but instead, his fingers only brushed Zhao's arm.

The crawling infected parted and Zhao walked down the middle of them. He stopped to drop one glow stick and pull another.

He took two steps further and cracked it.

A new bright glow cast over the Dragon.

He was sitting upon a throne of bodies, twisted and melded into a nightmarish shape. They were still alive, their jaws and eyes moving.

The Dragon sat atop of them. The metal dome around his head that robbed him of anything human. His tooled appendage rose up from his back, like a serpent watching Zhao's approach.

The Dragon grinned as Zhao came closer, and in the glow, his teeth looked yellow and black. "*My Chairman. I thank you for your attendance.*" His voice was hoarse, and much different than it had been.

Zhao came to stand at the base of the throne. He felt the infected circle around and tightened close to him.

Zhao stood straight, and his voice remained unbroken. "You have called, and I have come. It is time, Dragon. Time for you to do your duty to the People's Republic."

"My duty?" The Dragon's voice remained sharp and rigid. "What is my duty to *China?*"

Zhao stared into the Dragon's mechanical face. "Your duty is the same as mine. To live and breathe, and die if need be for the People's Republic."

The Dragon came down from the throne, and the bodies let out gasps of air as he stepped on them. His third arm snaked around over his shoulder. "And my people? The Kasher. Was that their duty? To die for China?"

Zhao was forced to step back as the Dragon came to the ground. He was larger than Zhao remembered; perhaps he'd grown. Zhao had no real understanding of what the Dragon was capable of, but now he stood inches taller than the premier, forcing Zhao to look up.

"What have you called me here for, *Dragon*?"

"That's not my name."

"Did you call me here *Dragon* to lay your pain before me and play upon my sympathies? Or is it your desire to terrify me?" Zhao held up the glow stick, casting a greenish glow onto the marble orb in the center of the Dragon's dome, and he could see his reflection staring back. "Are you the only one to suffer? I was there during the revolution. But before that, I saw my mother and friends starve to death. When the famine took hold, I ate what was handed to me. There was little food to go around, but there were many bodies. I suspect I was fed human. It had a strange taste I will never forget. But I ate it because I didn't want to die. I wanted to live. For China. For the People's Republic. To throw our decadent leaders from their towers and watch them fall to a screaming death for their avarice. I've known your hate. I've had it myself. So what is it then, Dragon? Will you kill me in such a way that you will never forget the sound of my screaming? Then do so. Avenge your pain upon my head, but when you are finished, go out and fight the enemies of the People's Republic, and bring us into a new age. Of power."

The glow stick's light began to fade, and Zhao knew that soon he would be stuck within darkness.

Within the dying light, Zhao took a step closer. "You and I are the same, *Dragon*. We live and die for the People's Republic. It's all we have."

WHEN ERKIN HAD COME, and after everyone else was dead, he found a woman cowering in the corner.

She was like him.

They'd made another one.

Erkin didn't know why, but it made him angry.

He squeezed her throat until she died.

Perhaps these were his children and no one else's?

177

Maybe that was it. Or maybe he was insane. He considered the possibility, but he wasn't particularly concerned.

But the dead girl hadn't been the only one.

There was another.

Alice Winters.

He knew the name. He could feel it in the hive mind.

But did she know him? He'd been quiet lately . . .

It didn't matter.

She would soon.

He walked within the darkness of the gymnasium. He couldn't see, but it wasn't necessary. The cronux viewed the world without eyes, and he could feel what they felt.

There was still blood on his hands as he pressed the door open, and he left a red handprint. The guards and soldiers aimed their rifles and focused their lights on him.

It may have been blinding, but the new eyes adjusted toward the brightness.

The security forces shouted as he stepped out of the gymnasium, the door closing behind him.

He didn't care what they had to say. No one would shoot him. No one would dare attempt to take his life.

He was the Dragon.

The hope of the People's Republic.

And their only chance at victory.

They all knew it.

Erkin squeezed his hand into a fist, and nearly all the creatures within the gymnasium curled up and died.

All except for the few at the entrance.

Hovercraft high above shined spotlights down on Erkin as he walked out into the open lot. With his extra eye, he could see everyone around him. The whole world.

Soldiers with guns, just beyond the fence, all waiting and watching.

All afraid.

The doors opened behind him and Zhao stumbled out. His glow stick had died, and Erkin had left him to find his way out.

Zhao raised up his hand and pulled the rebreather off. He coughed and waved his hand in the air. "*Stand down*. Stand down. The Dragon is with us."

A spotlight moved off of Erkin and to Zhao as he drew in closer.

"Open the gates! The Dragon has returned,." Zhao yelled as he walked past Erkin.

Erkin followed Zhao toward the entrance. Wu was there with a cigarette stuffed in his mouth, watching Erkin close in.

"Open up the gates!" Zhao called out again as he went over. The mechanized fencing shifted open, and Erkin followed behind.

Zhao's clothing was caked with the dust that was floating in the air, and it trickled off him as he moved.

"Director Wu," Zhao motioned him to come beyond the gate.

Wu was hesitant, but as the soldiers parted to give him room, he dropped his cigarette and snuffed it with his foot and entered, his hands tucked into his jacket pockets.

Inside, Zhao had stood face-to-face with him and offered his head. Erkin could respect that. But he had set his terms.

"I've written you a pardon for all that you've done here and for what you will do tonight," Zhao had said inside. *"I've left it in my desk drawer. Take whatever blood you need, and then stand with us against the enemies of China."*

"*My wife and daughter are dead,*" Erkin had said at the foot of his throne. *"I want blood, but not yours."*

Zhao had stared up at him, and without so much as blinking, had asked, *"Then who?"*

Wu had stared at Zhao as he came close, as if he were afraid to look at Erkin.

He should be.

The third arm snapped out like a spear and pierced Wu's shoulder. Inside, the fingers parted and Wu was hooked.

Wu had been the one that placed Erkin in the camp. The man with the burning cigarette who held Erkin's life in his hands.

But fate had changed.

Who had taken Erkin's family? Who had ordered the military into his town? Who had turned him into a monster?

He didn't know. Perhaps he never would.

But Wu would pay the price.

Erkin dragged Wu back toward the entrance as the man screamed in agony. Behind him Zhao held his hands up in the air.

"It's okay! It's okay!" Zhao yelled.

Erkin braced his legs and his third arm lifted Wu into the air. Erkin slammed Wu into the brick wall and shoved his hand onto Wu's jaw to keep him silent as Erkin spoke.

"Do you remember what you said to me when we first met?" Erkin asked.

Wu's gold-framed glasses had fallen off, and his eyes were now wide and staring at Erkin.

"You told me I would learn loyalty." Erkin leaned his head in, close enough that they almost touched. "Then you took everything from me."

The doors to the center opened and the few remaining infected reached their charred hands out.

Erkin shifted his weight and dragged Wu across the wall. He screamed as the infected grabbed and pulled him back into the darkness.

He was still screaming as Erkin turned around and walked toward Zhao. He saw Wu's gold-framed glasses, but stepped past them. Instead, he came to stand before Zhao, though he did not bow his head.

Instead he spoke.

"For the People's Republic."

22

ON A MOUNTAIN OVERLOOKING the dying city of Lahnzu, Alice sunk her hands into the dirt and crawled forward, but the dirt had turned to mud and it slipped between her fingers, and the climb was only getting steeper.

The fingers on her new arm, without so much as a command, began to extend and grow, adapting to the situation.

Voices screamed inside her mind.

"Stop," she said as she clawed the mud.

New voices came and others left. It built a pressure so thick inside her skull, she felt like her brain might push out her ears.

Alice pressed the clasp on her helmet and pulled it off. She dropped it into the mud and it rolled away, the internal lighting glowing in the dark.

She looked up into the sky. It was dark and the stars twinkled.

But when she looked over her shoulder, she could still see the city burning.

And she could still hear the voices screaming.

"*Get out,*" she begged again.

She'd left the city, and the creatures had dogged her, but she sent them away.

She needed to be alone. She needed to think.

But how could she? It was impossible with the screams so loud.

And Alice could see them all.

There was a woman dying now. One of the infected had grabbed her just as she was getting to her car.

An old man was stepping into the window frame. He jumped as the infected filled his room. It was the twentieth floor.

There were more.

So many.

She could taste the blood.

She rolled over and sat down on the dirt, her jaw going slack as she watched the city burn.

So many dead.

All because of her.

It was hard to think because she felt the pull, even here. The cronux were reaching for her, like a child for a mother's hand.

Something clicked inside her.

It was another scream.

A child.

Alice closed her eyes and focused, pushing her mind through the mess and drawing it into a needle point to find the one line within a scribble.

A boy was running, and Alice was behind him.

She was there to kill him.

She was in the mind of the infected, three in body, but one in mind, coming down upon the child.

But Alice stopped.

The bodies went tumbling forward, smashing into the ground. The collision made some of their bones break, and Alice felt it, but there was no pain.

The boy grabbed his mother's hand and she took him away.

Where they went, she didn't know. It was all vague like a face lit with a match at night.

There were others.

With all but a few holdouts, the security and the military were dead, and their bodies now belonged to Alice.

There were people rushing to get out, some running through the streets and others into cars or speeding trains leaving the city.

Half or more of the city was already dead.

The other half would soon follow.

Alice opened her eyes. Her mission was done, wasn't it?

She had gotten into the messaging room. She had aired it to all the people of China.

It had not been in their language, but she was sure they would understand.

"Submit or we will kill you all."

That was what she had been sent here to do.

And she had done that.

So why must more die?

It was hard to slide between the lines of control and to focus on anything in particular. So she wouldn't.

Within her mind's eye, she took the focus of the horde into her hand as if it were a stone. It changed shape and sometimes it was sharp and hurt to hold.

But Alice squeezed.

And if it were a stone with sharp edges, then Alice's hand would bleed.

She squeezed it anyway, and the sharp ridges cut her skin, but she squeezed all the harder.

Out there, in the world, some of the infected collapsed to their knees as their insides squeezed into knots. Their arms cracked and curled, and their heads twisted.

The parasites within them shriveled and popped.

They curled into empty husks and died.

Half the horde. All at once. Not enough to save the city.

But enough to give the people a chance to run.

Alice's eyes opened, but her vision was blurred. Blood ran out of her nose.

If the horde was a stone, then it was too heavy to hold for long, and she dropped it.

With that, her head rocked back and she breathed in deep.

It was the boy that had helped her focus. Why was that?

She fell back and looked up into the sky. She closed her eyes and breathed even though it was no longer needed.

The boy . . .

The boy . . .

The boy . . .

And now she could feel the Archon's presence coming. He was with her once more, in mind if not in body, and his heavy hand was on her shoulder, pulling her back into the abyss.

But there was one final thought as her mind went dark.

Her eyes flared open.

Eli.

23

JOHN OPENED the door and stepped into the private viewing room. He knew it must be something important if Roles didn't want to risk sending it directly to his desk.

Roles was standing at attention. "Mr. President."

"Might not be able to say that for long. I just got off the phone with McIntyre. No deal. No compromise. He wants me out and I'm starting to wonder why I'm fighting him for it."

"Did you hear the plan they want to impose?"

"Yes, and they're idiots. If any of them had half a brain, I'd gladly hand the job to them. So what's this then?" John gestured toward the screen.

"We've intercepted two videos from Chinese communications and authenticated them. They're Alice."

John took a sharp breath as he felt icy fingers wrap around his heart.

"All right then, let me see them." He sat down at the table and Roles came down alongside him.

Roles had a small command board in front of him, and he punched in numbers. "We believe this first vid is from some civilian with a camera, but it's hard to say." He pressed a button.

A grainy video with dull colors began. The angle was coming from somewhere up high and angled down toward a street. A wave of Chinese security forces had taken up cover behind two cars. They fired at something off camera, but the view shifted to look. Waves of infected rushed down the street. Some tumbling over as the bullets hit them, but others rushing directly over top of them.

The vid panned back and forth before it snapped at one angle.

A woman in American CAG walked down the street, her rifle up and firing.

The vid panned back again to the forces and they staggered back as infected slammed into the cars, some leaping over and grabbing men. The security teams broke and ran.

The vid shifted again and it was back on Alice rushing down the street with a four-legged beast galloping alongside her.

A fat, dead face filled the screen suddenly, and whoever was recording fell back as a creature climbed into the room with them.

The vid went black.

"What the hell did they do to her?" John asked. "Have you seen anything like that? Them using weapons?"

Roles shook his head. "No, I haven't."

John rubbed the bridge of his nose. "You said there was another vid?"

Roles gave John a flat look. "There is, but it's not easy to see."

"Just play it."

Roles reached over and pressed a few keys.

The screen flashed and lit up again.

It was a low-angled camera set inside some communications room. Alice stood in full CAG at the edge. A massive creature on two legs with four arms stood at her side. It was so large that half of it was off the screen. Dead men with cold, gray faces and twitching insectile limbs crouched and crawled around, but their attention was forward on the camera.

John felt his chest tighten with every step as she approached the screen.

She stopped and stared at the camera. Her CAG was damaged and scarred. One whole sleeve was missing and she had a long rigid arm that looked like it had two elbows. The creatures followed close to loom over her shoulders. She pressed the clasp on her helmet. Air popped as it lifted and Alice took it off.

Her blonde hair looked wet and clung to her face. Her skin was pale and wax-like. Her eyes had a deep gaze.

Tears rolled down her cheeks as she stared.

John reached over Roles and hit a button. "I've seen enough. I don't want to hear her voice. What happened?"

Roles cleared his throat. "She warned the Chinese forces to give up their arms and join. She said that they don't all need to die."

John gave a labored sigh and shook his head. "None of this makes any damn sense. Are they taking prisoners now?"

Roles shook his head again. "Honestly, I have no idea what's going on there."

John took a deep breath. "Roles. That isn't my daughter."

"I know."

"It's wearing her skin, but it's not her. It shouldn't exist. What can you do about it?"

"If you want it to end, I can get to work on it."

John nodded his head. "I owe Alice that much. Whatever *this* is, it's not my daughter and it shouldn't exist." John stiffened his back and looked down at his watch. "Any further update on Moller?"

"No. The last report I received was that she has been picked up and is currently being transported back to base. The team there will prep her for our meeting."

John stood up and adjusted his jacket. "All right then. I have a scheduled conference call with the European Federation delegates. I'll see you in the meeting."

Miles sat down at a conference desk with the president of the United States. He put his hands under the table so that when he squeezed his fists together, no one noticed.

Somehow, by some bad roll of the dice, Miles had found himself appointed Head of the Cronux Task Force for the president of the United States.

Roles had been the one to give him the news, saying it with a face as flat as a board.

"Me?" Miles had asked him, grabbing Roles by the arm. *"Why the hell are you putting me in front of it?"*

Roles had looked down at Miles' hands and back up. His gaze was strong enough that Miles took a step back.

"Do you think we'd choose a British TV personality if we had someone else?"

So that's why Miles was here, wringing his hands beneath the table.

Because they didn't have anyone better.

He supposed he always just assumed that the president of the United States had the phone number of every noteworthy expert in the world, and could summon them like some bureaucratic genie out of a lamp, complete with a solid-colored tie, a bland sense of humor, and a strict policy on formal wear.

Miles was trying his best, but deadly serious and formal wear weren't really his thing.

The secretary had told him he should at least wear a tie if he was going to keep meeting with the president. So he went and bought one across the street at one of the gift shops.

Now he was wearing that tie in his first official meeting as Head of the Cronux Task Force.

He couldn't help but notice that John Winters' tie was a solid dark blue.

Kevin had one on too, gray with black stripes.

Even the damn communist had a red tie on with a white button-up shirt. The pinky, pencil-necked bastard had it buttoned up high enough to strangle a normal man.

Miles glanced down to his own tie.

It was blue with a lot of miniature American flags on it.

Dammit, it had felt presidential at the time, but on second thought, a Brit with a flashy tie that screamed *American* came off tacky.

He sighed as he looked up to see if anyone noticed, but thank God, they were all more focused with the collapse of the world to notice the shitty tie.

Miles glanced down at it once more. Sure, bit too American for a Brit, but he was trying to support the team, right?

Ahh hell, bow ties were always more his thing. Big, goofy ass ones too.

He really was a fish out of water, but he supposed he wasn't the only one.

The communist was seated across from him, and bouncing in his seat, itching for a cigarette.

Kevin was next to him, a wide-eyed stare like he just took a good kick to the balls.

Miles wanted to poke him in the ribs and say, *"Wouldn't kill you to blink, mate,"* but he didn't feel like it was the right time for shitty jokes.

Now John Winters though, he was the kind of hard-faced bastard that was built to manage an empire. His back was straight, his hair combed, and even though he had his jacket off and his sleeves rolled up, his tie was still on tight.

If someone carved his face out of stone and sat it along a shelf of Roman emperors, it wouldn't look out of place.

Even still, Miles could see the lines and dark circles around his eyes.

Not to mention the discolored vein poking out from under his sleeve from shooting up too much juice.

Miles felt like he hadn't slept in days, but God only knows how John Winters was still up and walking.

Yeah, he looked a bastard all right, but sometimes you need a bastard in charge, especially one that had the appearance that they knew what they were doing.

Do you think he knows what he's doing?

Ahh, there's that little shit-talking voice.

If John Winters knows what he's doing, then why is his staff cut down to the bone? Why the hell does he have a task force made out of goofballs?

And why would he have put you in charge of anything?

"Because there's no one else better," Miles mumbled.

Everyone in the room looked at him.

"I was, uhh—" He glanced around. "Just an itch in my throat." He grinned and everyone looked away. Fucking hell, it felt like an oven. Miles wanted to loosen his tie, but how could he do that when John Winters had his tight and ironed?

Kevin tapped his fingers on the table and smiled wide. "So when are they calling?"

John Winters glanced down at his watch and then folded his hands back together again. "They were due to call five minutes ago."

Oh, right. The meeting wasn't about Miles' insecurities, it was about the blonde. Moller, up in New York, and she was due to give a report as soon as they had her treated.

"Keeping the president of the United States waiting, ehh? Must be an important lady." Miles grinned.

The president flashed him a look but did nothing else. Miles glanced across the table and the others avoided eye contact.

Miles let the smile slip off and grabbed for his water.

John took a deep breath, and they all turned to look at him. "Everyone, I know we're all nervous, but I want to make something clear before we begin." He waited long enough to look each of them in the eyes. "My daughter was one of the first to encounter the creatures —I've never dealt with cronux. They're still hard for me to comprehend. You're all here because you have first-hand experience and better insight than me. When this conference finally begins, do not hesitate to express your concerns or ask any questions."

Miles nodded and there were murmured agreements.

He took a deep breath. "I was also waiting until after the meeting to inform you all, but it seems we have a bit of time now." John hesitated. "The chimera are almost certainly mixing in with our populations."

"What?" Miles said without thinking.

"We quarantined New York City, and began evacuations, but there's only so much we can do when trying to move a population of ten million people. There aren't enough places to put people. The more we slow down, the more people will be left inside with the creatures, and they've already broken our defensive lines several times."

John Winters' voice was so flat that it betrayed how sharp the words were. Miles felt like he couldn't breathe.

"They're mixing in here. It's going to spread," he said more to himself than anyone else.

Marat raised his hand like a student in class. "Mr. John Winters—"

"You can just call me John," he said with a dull shake of his head.

Marat smiled and hissed in some breath. He looked up toward the ceiling as if considering what to say. "I think there is no answer, but stop evacuations."

"Hmm?" Kevin asked him.

"Close fence and be careful with those that already passed."

Kevin shook his head. "We can't do that, there are millions of people still in there."

"How many millions?" Marat asked with a curious glance.

"He said it," Kevin gestured toward John. "Ten million."

"American people are three hundred and fifty million. Much more than ten."

"What? You just want to leave them to die?" Kevin lifted his lip.

Marat looked honestly taken aback. "No, no. I don't want them to die. I want us to live."

Miles shook his head. "Mate, this isn't the Soviet Union, we can't do that kind of thing here. We just have to work out some new ideas."

Marat nodded his head. "You were in Soviet Union during this disaster?"

Miles nodded. "All up and down it, even rode the rail. Was lovely until it wasn't."

"You heard the people scream?" Marat's voice had an edge.

Miles huffed. "Mate, I told you I was there. What do you think?"

"Do you think American people scream different than Soviet?"

Marat's eyes held a cold stare. "Do they bleed a different color? We all die same way."

Miles pointed a finger at Marat and glanced to John. "Well this bastard's awfully chatty all of the sudden."

"He's not wrong though." John crossed his arms. "And neither are you."

"*Fucking hell.*" Miles decided he didn't give a shit anymore, and loosened his tie. "We really talking about leaving a few million people to get eaten?"

"No." John shook his head. "I am thinking we need to move up the time frame on deploying the military."

"What's that, mate—err—Mr. President?"

"The Navy is getting into position to pepper Long Beach, and deploy the Marines. We're going to dig them out by the root, but there are still civilians there."

"One thing though." Kevin held up a finger. "These things *keep* changing. The military needs to be ready for that."

"They will be informed." John sighed. "But we need Moller's report."

The door to the conference room opened and Roles stepped in. "Sorry, Mr. President, there has been some technical interference, but we're connecting with the base now." He took a seat at the table.

The monitor on the wall flipped on. It fizzled and popped with gray static.

"What's going on here?" John gestured toward it.

Roles shook his head. "They're reporting signal interference. The reasoning is unclear."

A man in a beige jumpsuit—the kind worn under hazmat gear—stepped into view. "*Mr. President?*" The man looked off screen and said something that wasn't clear, and refocused on the camera. "*Mr. President, can you hear me?*"

John frowned. "We can hear you, but you're not who we were expecting."

"*I'm Eric Trenton, I'm a civilian contractor acting as lead coordinator, and mission specialist for the deployment of the tomb armor system. I have red condition security clearance."* The man had his chin up, but had his brow wrinkled in concern.

"Mr. Trenton, I was under the impression we would be speaking to agent Moller. She conducted a sensitive mission within New York, and we were alerted that she was retrieved and being brought back to base."

"*Sir.*" Trenton's gaze flicked off camera again. *"There was a problem."*

Roles frowned deeply and cleared his throat. "Mr. Trenton. I'm sure you understand that the president's time is precious. Please speak plainly and clearly."

Trenton bobbed his head up. *"There was a—"* He looked down and back up again. *"There was a suit breach and she soaked in a terminal amount of radiation. It's a wonder she got as far as she did. Her geo-tracker indicated she had traveled some fifty miles. But the timing indicators are misfiring, so it's unclear how long she was—"*

"Mr. Trenton," John said with some force. "Focus please. You need to inform us of the state of agent Moller. Is she incapacitated?"

He rubbed a hand through his hair. He stared at something off the camera. *"I'm trying. It's just—"* He glanced back. *"She should be dead, but she keeps demanding to report. I think it's all that's keeping her alive."*

"Put her on. Right now," Roles snapped.

Trenton shook his head. *"It's not pretty. But here."*

The camera lifted and bobbed and snapped down onto a table. It focused on a bed and a woman with graying skin.

Roles inhaled sharply, and John mumbled, *"Christ. Is she—?"*

Moller's head rolled to look at the camera. Her eyes were large and puffy, her face was blistered, and her lips were dark purple.

"Report . . . I have to—"

"*Moller!*" Roles shouted. "We're here."

Miles watched Roles grip the table and come up from the chair.

"Gah-h . . ." she struggled to breathe.

"Take your time, Moller. Just breathe," John said with a father's patience.

She took two long, raspy breaths and spoke. *"Gate. They have a gate."* She rolled her head back onto the pillow and went silent.

Miles held up a finger. "Did she just . . .?"

John ignored him. "Mr. Trenton, is Moller still alive?"

The camera snapped up and Trenton angled it at his face, but he was looking away. *"She's still alive, but with the amount of radiation she took, she won't likely survive the night."*

"Unacceptable!" Roles barked. "I'm sending a trauma and a mechanized surgery team."

Trenton's eyes widened. *"As project leader, her care falls under my command, we'd need proper LBA agreements before we can replace organs."*

"I'm assuming emergency control of the patient and all legal liabilities." Roles thrusted a finger at the screen. *"Do not let her die."*

Trenton bobbed his head.

John spoke with a much calmer voice. "Is there anything else you can inform us of, Mr. Trenton?"

"No, Mr. President, there is not."

"Keep us updated on agent Moller's status. That'll be all for now." Without waiting for a reply, John reached over and pushed a button ending the call and making the screen turn black.

Roles stood up from his chair, and adjusted his jacket. "I have to order the medical teams there. I'll be back in fifteen minutes."

John nodded and motioned toward the door. Roles huffed out.

"I guess they're close?" Miles asked.

John shook his head. "Apparently. You heard what she said though, there's a gate open." John made a confused gesture with his hand. "What does that mean and what do we do about it?"

"Fucking hell this is awful." Miles rubbed his nose and closed his eyes. He glanced up. "Well, this one's on you comrade. Kevin here and I haven't seen a gate."

"That's not exactly true, I saw one in a video."

Closing his eyes again and giving an exhausted nod, Miles said, "Yes, Kevin, you saw one in a video. You might be the world's leading expert on gates, comrade." Miles gestured toward Marat.

Marat looked up with a somber glare. "Yes, I have seen gate. Two gates."

"I read the reports about Felicity. They said that the systems affected communication signals," John said.

Marat nodded. "We have similar problems on our project. Some signals disrupt technology and we have to, ehh, harden systems to protect from disruptions."

Miles put one arm over the back of his chair and the other leaning on the table. "What kind of disruptions?"

"They make, ehh . . ." Marat gestured as if he was holding an invisible ball and frowned. "Mechanical failure. Not power loss but, *dut-dut-dut-dut.*" He chopped his hand in the air a few times.

"We talking hiccups here, mate? The system struggling to get going?" Miles asked.

"Like a car with a bad battery?" Kevin added.

Marat nodded his head and pointed at Kevin. "Like this. Not dead. Only hiccup."

John crossed his arms. "Were you involved in that process much? Could you replicate the research for hardening systems?"

Marat nodded. "I was not involved, but we work together. I understand a large piece of it."

Miles glanced at John. "What are you thinking?"

John exhaled. "Moller told us that there was a gate functioning in the area. But before that, the base reported that her ship went down for unknown reasons. I wonder if that damn thing coming on made the ship sputter."

"Like an EMP?" Kevin asked. "But how come we didn't see anything like that before?"

Miles pointed at Marat. "He said it, mate. They had the problem they just hardened the systems to deal with it in development. All the other developments surely had the same problem."

John looked to Marat. "After this meeting we're going to get you in touch with some of our research and development teams in an advisory position." John looked at Kevin and Miles. "We're going to get you two in touch with our emergency response coordinators and you're going to inform them everything you know and what to look out for."

Miles nodded and looked to Kevin. "I guess we better get to it."

"Not just yet. We intercepted a few videos from the Chinese. I think it's important that you watch them. They're of my daughter, and I don't care to see them again, so you'll have to wait until Roles comes back. He only has them on hard file for the moment." John sighed and stood up. "I'm sure Roles will be able to answer any other questions for you. I'll be waiting for your reports."

John gave them all a nod and headed out of the room.

Miles stood up and loosened his tie more. "Enough of that nonsense." He tossed it across the room.

"Feel better?" Kevin asked.

"No, but at least I feel less like an idiot." Miles put his hands on the back of his head and paced the room. It helped when he was stressed. "Who the hell did I piss off to somehow be in charge of an alien task force for the president of the United States? There isn't even an American in the damn room."

"I was promised citizenship," Marat said as he dug at his inside jacket pocket.

"Ain't that just the icing on the cake? The communist is the only American."

Marat pulled out a cigarette and stuffed it into his mouth.

"Really? You need to smoke again? You can't possibly need that many cigarettes, comrade. Why don't you just start eating tar to save some time?"

Kevin closed his eyes and threw his head back. "Leave him alone. He's as stressed as the rest of us."

Marat lit the cigarette and took a puff. He nervously tapped his finger on the table as he stared at a wall. *"The cow jumps over the fence, so the farmer frowns,"* he mumbled.

"What?" Kevin raised an eyebrow.

Marat gave an exhausted sigh and shook his head.

The door opened and they all looked over. Roles came in, and his face was even stiffer than usual, but his tie was still on straight. He took two steps in when he saw Miles' tie on the floor. He glanced toward Miles.

Miles snorted. "I can put it back on if you'd like."

"No, just sit down." Roles pointed to a chair as he moved toward the monitor. "You've all seen the first video?"

Miles made a face as he took a seat. "Sure did, but I don't know what the hell to make of it. I've never seen one of those things act like that."

"None of us have." Roles plugged something into the monitor then typed in commands on the keyport. It started playing as he moved to take a seat.

Miles leaned back and watched as Alice Winters came alive on screen in some kind of battle. She moved just like a soldier, taking aim and firing. He even noticed small gestures she made with her hand that sent the cronux running. And they all moved in some strange pattern. Like an ocean come to life, rising and falling in waves against her movements.

Was that what they were going to have to deal with now? Something with a brain that knew how to wield them like a sword?

"*Shit . . .*" Miles hissed.

As one video ended, another began. This time in a room and she approached the camera. Miles watched with keen interest as the others bowed up and followed her with their heads.

She lifted her helmet, and Miles saw her pale face wet with tears. He leaned in.

She began speaking, but he didn't hear it. He was focused on her eyes.

Miles glanced around the room to see if they were seeing the same thing as him.

But just by the looks on their faces, he could tell that they weren't.

"Why is she crying?" Kevin asked.

No one answered.

He turned back and saw the tears drip down her eyes.

Miles was a con man. He played on people's emotions. He knew how to give them what they wanted.

And he knew how to read a face.

She's trapped.

He knew that by looking into her eyes.

Miles looked away again, his eyes searching across the table as his mind worked.

The vid ended and Kevin spoke, "God that was horrifying. Do you think that—"

"What's the plan?" Miles interrupted.

Roles exhaled and folded his hands together on the table. "The president is going to have a meeting with the Chinese ambassador. They're in a more difficult position than they were before, and they're more amicable to communications."

"Yeah, yeah, and?" Miles said, tapping his foot.

"They want to make sure we have nothing to do with it, and that it won't start a war if they kill her," Roles said, his face flat. "The president is going to put them in contact with a Soviet kill team that can—"

"No. I need to talk to him." Miles came up from his seat and moved toward the door. Roles said something to his back, but he pulled the door open and stepped into the hallway.

He glanced either way down the halls, but he still had a shit understanding of where he was. The hallway on the left had a painting on the wall of a log cabin that looked vaguely familiar.

Good enough.

Miles hurried in that direction as Roles came out of the room and called at Miles' back. "Where the hell are you going?"

Miles went to a cross in the hallways and looked down each side. "Who the hell's idea was it to make every damn hallway look the same?" He saw the bust of Abraham Lincoln that had stared him down before. He snapped his fingers and went that direction. "Mr. Lincoln," Miles said with a nod as he passed.

There were doors at the end of the hallway. They opened up and the president's secretary came out.

Miles picked up his pace, and she gasped as he came closer.

"Is he in there?" Miles asked.

"He's in a meeting, you have to—"

"Miles, wait!" Roles shouted.

Miles pushed in past the secretary and saw John Winters behind his desk.

Miles cleared his throat. "Mr. President, we have to talk."

The secretary grabbed his arm. "You have to go, he has a meeting!"

Miles pulled away. "It's about your daughter. We need to talk before you make any plans."

John frowned at him. "You picked a bad time, I'm thirty seconds away from a call with the Chinese ambassador."

"He can wait." Miles held up a finger.

The secretary looked at John but he shook his head. "Fine, let me hear what you have to say."

Roles came into the room a second later, his eyes like daggers at Miles.

Miles glanced at him, then back to John. "Listen, ties, meetings, presidential titles, I don't know a damn thing about any of that. It's not me. But I *do* know people."

"What the hell is your point?" Roles asked him, breathing a little hard.

Miles approached John's desk and pointed at his face. "I saw Alice's eyes. I couldn't hear a damn word she said, but I didn't need to. Her eyes told me all I needed to know. She's trapped in there."

John shook his head. "That might be true. I don't know. But right now she's out there leading an army against the Chinese. What can we do?"

Miles planted both hands on the desk and leaned in. "I have a plan, I mean, I know a guy."

"Who?" John asked.

Miles grinned. "The most dangerous man on Earth."

EPILOGUE

ENDO KNELT in the center of a Soviet cell. The concrete floor was cold and the walls were bare but for patches of peeling white paint.

His synthetic intestine slithered inside his gut. The edges rubbed his stomach lining with incredible pain.

He took in a breath, and he exhaled.

The room was cold, but it was silent.

It gave him time to think, and to empty his mind.

The pain was terrible, but even that worked to sharpen his focus and drag his thoughts away from his life.

With each breath he took, he could smell paint.

Within his mind's eye, he saw a brush dip into black paint and trace across a white canvas. Fat drips of paint streaked down from the strokes.

He could not remember his father's face, but he remembered his warm smile as he said:

"Not all things are intended. But that does not make them ugly."

The thought made Endo warm, and it dulled the pain.

The Soviets had interrogated him, and he had hid nothing, but he did not think of such things now.

He sought only to empty himself, and, if possible, to reach deep inside and smell the paint upon his father's canvas.

His ear twitched as he heard steps coming toward his room.

They always fed him once a day, and now was not the time.

Perhaps they had come to execute him? Or maybe he would be given back to the Japanese government to be dealt with?

Neither concerned him.

Not all things were intended, but that did not make them ugly.

Endo kept his back to the door as the locks turned and opened. He never rose when they entered, and he wouldn't now unless they commanded him.

If they chose to enter and shoot him in the back of the head, he would do nothing to stop them.

"Kota Endo," a deep voice growled.

Endo looked up. He turned to see Grand Marshal Garin with his synthetic jaw staring at him. Two soldiers in CAG stood behind him.

But there was a datapad in his hand.

"We have a message for you." Garin spoke Russian, but Endo understood. Garin held the datapad out.

Endo rose to his feet and bowed his head in respect as he took the datapad. He looked down and saw Miles Westwood's smiling face beaming back.

Miles held up a hand. *"Listen, it's a long story, but we've already had a chat with the Japanese government and the Soviet forces. The Japanese authorized us to contact you and the Soviets agreed to release you."*

"Why? I don't understand."

"Mate, I'm here with the president of the United States." Miles moved and got alongside John Winters, who only nodded. *"We've got a favor to ask."*

Endo glanced toward the officer in the room, then back to the screen. "What?"

"First." Miles raised his eyebrows. *"Do you still have your CAG?"*

Somehow, in that moment, Endo heard his father's voice again, as clear as it had ever been.

"Not all things are intended. But that does not make them ugly."

WHAT'S NEXT?

Want to know the latest on the *Reality Bleed* series?

Join our Facebook group to talk *Reality Bleed* and keep up-to-date on everything that's happening.

FAILED STATES OF AMERICA

REALITY BLEED BOOK 10

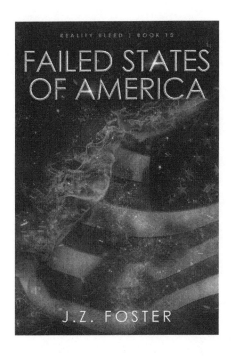

ABOUT J.Z. FOSTER

J.Z. Foster is a writer originally from Ohio. He spent several years in South Korea where he met and married his wife.

He received the writing bug from his mother, NYTimes best-selling author, Lori Foster.

Check out his other books and let him know how you like them!

Write him an email at:
JZFoster@JZFoster.com

WINTER GATE PUBLISHING

Want to stay up to date on the latest from Winter Gate Publishing? Follow us on Facebook at Facebook.com/WinterGatePublishing to know more!

Made in the USA
Middletown, DE
21 October 2022

13182749R00128